The Heirs of Lilian

THE QUEEN'S RING

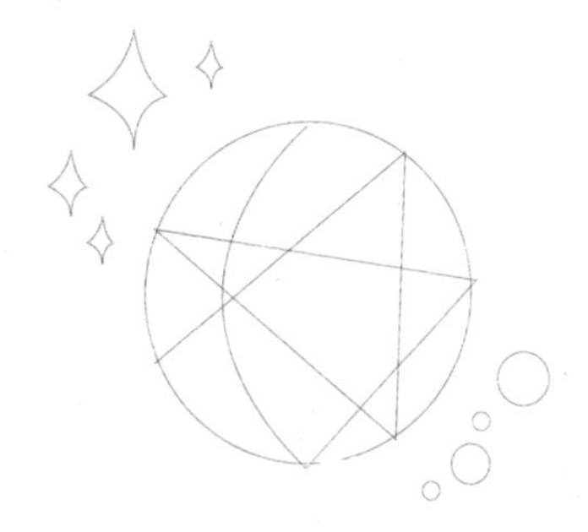

First published in Republic of Korea in 2020.
LABOBOOKS, Gyeonggi-do Bucheon-si Hohyeon-ro 467beon-gil
33-5, first floor(ROK)

Book design by Sung Kyeol and Anne Y. Chang.

ISBN 979-11-965340-0-4

Printed in Republic of Korea by Yewon Printing

labo.libros@gmail.com
Tel. 031-882-4304

The Heirs of Lilian

THE QUEEN'S RING

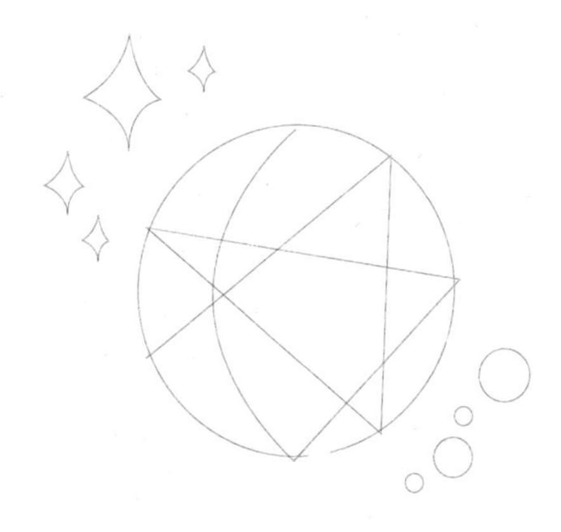

Anne Y. Chang

LABO BOOKS

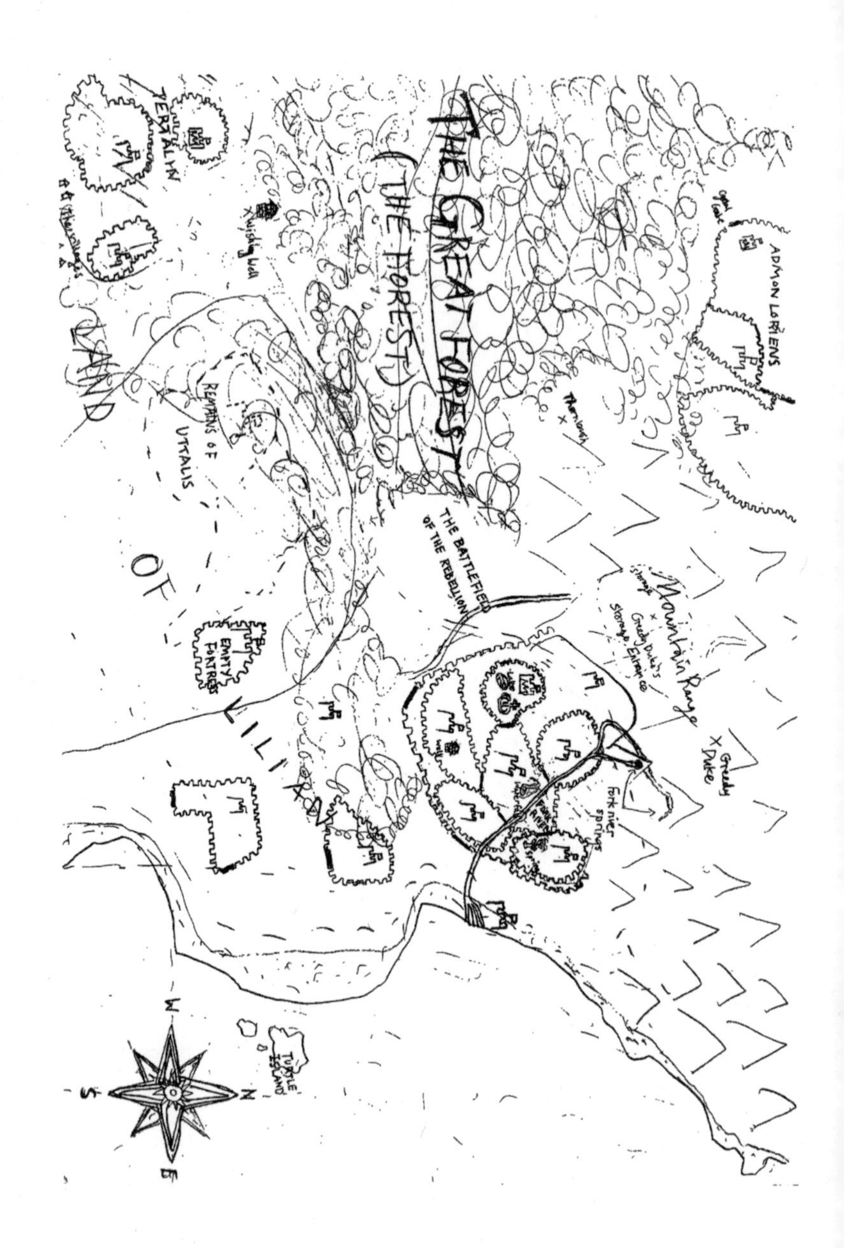

A brief map that Anne drew

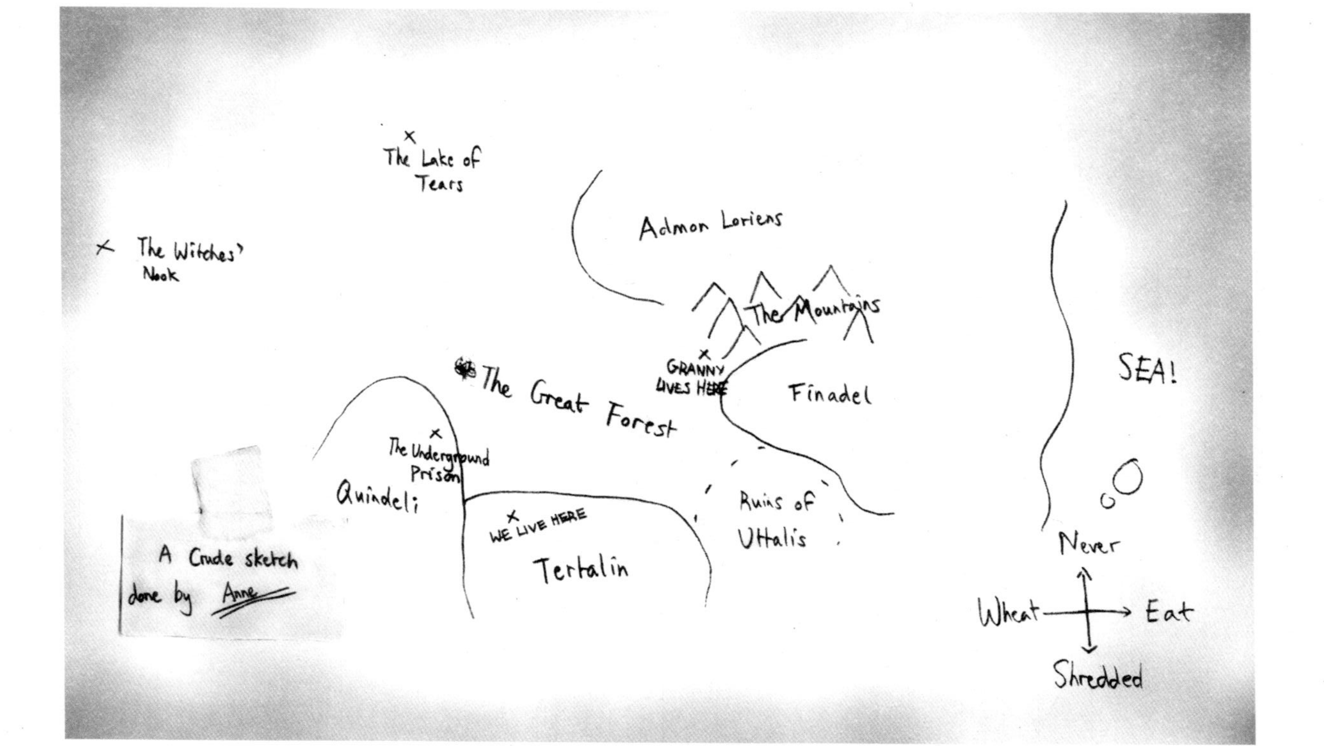
The Lake of Tears
The Witches' Nook
Admon Loriens
The Mountains
GRANNY LIVES HERE
The Great Forest
Finadel
SEA!
The Underground Prison
Quindeli
WE LIVE HERE
Tertalin
Ruins of Uttalis
A Crude sketch done by Anne
Never
Wheat
Eat
Shredded

I wrote this book for Grace,
dearest sister.

Prologue

The lamp, the lamp, the lamp ...

He stopped in front of the wall, his head full of thoughts.

A descendant of Feridan had it, he knew. He had met her a few hours ago. But could it be ... could it really be the lamp of Tieral?

He had to take hold, he had to take hold of it, the lamp ...

But the price? Is it worth so much?

Nothing is worth more! Certainly, that is the most valuable thing of all. Should that foul woman deserve to keep it any longer?

No, but there must be another way; a better one, not with so much loss and separation. After all, there is a guilt feeling about this thought, so it must not be good. Or maybe, he was imagining this guilt? For, he persuaded himself, what is there to be guilty about? But what, then, might be that which is called guilt?

There is no other way. There is no price too big; that is the most valuable of all things.

Then, was it even more valuable than family? Than friends? Than his kingdom and name, and future? Than love?

He hesitated.

Don't think! How many times have you considered, yet decided that the lamp is what is important?

A voice seemed to whisper in his ear, coaxing him. The voice of his thoughts ...

"Then why do I feel so uncomfortable?" he whispered to himself. "I am not sure what the meaning of Tieral is, if the price for it does not seem right. And the price will not only affect me, but also my daughters – and my dear Queen."

This is selfishness. Think of all the blessings your people will be deprived of, just because you think only of your family!

But is this really for your people?

It was unrightfully stolen from the King of the East, so long ago.

"Even if it weren't for them," he concluded, "I'd be doing my duty in returning it."

He shook his head to rid the endlessly repetitive argument raging inside. It was giving him a headache, like his head was being split into two.

There was no turning back; his plot was spun and now it had hatched.

"Love," he said, answering the scrawl on one side of the wall that he hadn't cared to look at.

A stately man wrapped in a plain grey cloak opened the door and looked out of the stables. His face was hidden under the hem of his hood, and with further caution a ragged grey scarf was wrapped around. He looked up at the grey sky that was starting to be tinged with the orange glow of the sun. Dawn was beginning to break through the twilight.

The man quickly stepped out, locking the door behind him. He passed the flourishing carrot patches, closing the gate behind him. He hurriedly walked into the woods. He quickened his steps until he was half running, reaching the oak tree and slipping inside.

It was very dark, but he didn't need a torch to lead him.

Once inside the palace, the man passed by the bookshelves and opened the door into the corridor. Reaching a door, he eased it open with only a slight creak and crept in, his hand reaching for the small, black box ...

— CHAPTER ONE —

One Autumn Afternoon

The two girls squealed with laughter as they blindly sprayed water at each other.

"Hey!" said Anne, wiping away the water from her eyes as Grace concentrated her blows there. "Stop! Stop! I didn't intend to get wet ... I don't like the soggy feeling."

Anne covered her face with her hands, half laughing and half sobbing, in order to prevent the water going up her nose as Grace stood waiting for her to remove her hands. Anne peeked, and Grace started spraying again. Anne just quit covering her face and started splashing everywhere without seeing where Grace was. There was a colossal splash somewhere to her right, and Anne opened her eyes to see Grace had slipped and fallen into the water. She laughed as Grace stood up, grinning. Grace waded towards land shivering, while Anne followed her, never ceasing to laugh.

"Quit smirking, Anne," Grace said as she waited for Anne to get out. "Ha, ha, yeah, I was terrifically funny."

They sat on a rock for some while to regain their energy for more play, gazing as the sun weaved in between the tops of the fir trees to reflect its light upon the shimmering waters of the ravine they had just played in.

"I guess it is autumn for sure," commented Anne, shivering slightly as a cool breeze rustled the fir tree leaves. "I love autumn. But I also like summer. I like wearing short-sleeved shirts, the loose-fitting ones with sleeves coming down just above the elbow, if you get what I mean."

"Holy Lilian, do you mean it?" said Grace, putting one cold, wet hand on the back of Anne's neck.

"If Lilian is holy, you shouldn't use his name like that," said Anne, jerking away from the hand. "But, what? – Mean what?"

"Holy Belmer – surely you know!" said Grace, with a wide grin that made her cheeks look very chubby. " '*If you get what I mean*'?! Ha. Honestly, do you think there would be a single thing in your mind that I can't read? Holy Tepiraniel!"

"I thought you'd already admitted that you'd been fibbing about reading my mind when I got grumpy because you weren't telling the truth," said Anne rather grumpily. "I'll guess next, you'll be saying, 'Holy Adren, Holy Fridence, Holy –' "

"Okay, okay, fine," said Grace, leaning over upon her hands and knees. "Let's say ... let's say it's the other way around. *You* can read my mind. What am I thinking right now?"

"That you are going to catch another frog to let loose in our room to see Mum's expression," said Anne with a slight frown as she scrutinized Grace.

"Exactly," said Grace, beaming. "And you are not going to tell, are you?"

"Might," said Anne uncertainly.

"Augh, man, Anne, it spoils the fun!" said Grace, nearly knocking Anne over with one of her clumsy slaps on the head. "Okay, then, you're a telly-tale, satisfied?" she said, trying another tactic.

"Now you've secured the fact that I'm going to tell," said Anne rather heatedly, but grudgingly breaking into a smile as Grace tried to put on a cute, pleading face.

"Now, you're wondering if there's a towel, right?" said Grace, who seemed to have come to a conclusion that Anne would not tell on her since she smiled and already getting up to catch the frog.

"Yeah," Anne said, shivering again. "I do want to play, but you've sprayed water up my nose, so I have to have more time to recover. And Grace, I don't think it's a very considerate thing to do to Mum when her birthday is only two weeks away ..."

Anne sat on the rock watching Grace splashing and slipping to catch some frogs. She suddenly heard a snap behind her, as if someone had stepped on a twig, someone making their way towards her. Standing up, she peered into the dark fir trees. She felt fear clamping down upon her shoulders in a swift moment, and she instinctively reached for the sword lying in its scabbard, next to where she had been sitting. The fir tree branches began to quiver and shake, and though she heard another great splash behind her, Anne didn't care to look at Grace slipping yet another time. Then –

Crack!

As the branches gave way, Anne pulled out the sword and nearly drew it upon the elderly woman in the hooded cloak. Anne immediately dropped the sword, and it clattered to the ground. She was breathing rapidly.

"Sorry," she said to the elderly woman, who looked concerned. Anne stooped down to put the sword back in its scabbard and sat down, moving up to make space for the granny to sit down. Below, Grace had just realized the granny had come, and she looked up to wave before crouching back down again.

"I brought you a towel," remarked the granny, with the air of someone who says '*The weather is good*', peering about the tree tops before producing a large, red towel that had the word 'splash' sowed in with golden thread, which she wrapped around Anne.

"Thank you," said Anne, pulling the towel closer around herself. "By the way, Granny, do you think I should tell Mum about what Grace is about to do, or not? Mum's birthday is only two weeks away."

The granny took one look down at Grace, who was still slipping and splashing after performing some wild, grasping gestures, and guessed exactly what Grace was planning to do to 'Mum'.

"What if you let Grace choose if she will really frighten Her Majesty the Queen or not?" said the granny thoughtfully. "She might, after all, *fail* to catch a frog."

As they sat there, the sun appeared over the tree tops and shone upon them directly, the warm sunlight soaking through their skin.

Just then, Anne heard an ear-splitting screech, like the sound of an eagle. As she looked up, a shadow passed across them as a huge bird high up in the sky swooped across from one side of the ravine to the other. It looked like a gigantic eagle, since it was the size of a close-up robin even though it was so far up in the sky. Just as Anne was thinking it must be a golden eagle, the sun reflected upon it, and the eagle glinted in the light as if it was actually made of solid gold.

The granny watched Anne open her mouth with surprise, and she smiled.

"Do you see that golden eagle?" she asked Anne. Anne tore her gaze from the disappearing eagle to look at the granny.

"What ... was that? What does it all mean?"

"It means that something special is about to happen, Anne," said the granny, standing up and brushing her cloak off. "Something special, all over again."

Below, Grace yelped, then called up to them, "I caught a frog, but I let it go! How was I to know it's actually as slimy as it looks?!"

— CHAPTER TWO —

A Lost Ring

"Cockadoodledoo! Cockadoodledoo!"

The rooster alarm clock started off crowing, announcing six o'clock in the morning. The girls woke up and automatically made their beds. With closed, sleepy eyes, Grace grabbed the brush lying on her desk and began attacking her bushy hair that was made up into a rat's nest by her bad sleeping habits and then tied her hair up. Anne just managed to tie her hair without any brushing, but Grace spotted her and made her brush it. Anne's hair broke Grace's brush, and after both had changed into their dresses, they headed downstairs to eat breakfast.

"My friend asked me the other day why we eat cereal for breakfast, not some posh muffins and cake, or something like that," said Grace while she tried to slide down the staircase banister and failed like every other morning.

"So, what did you say?" Anne asked. They reached the doors to the dining hall, where a doorkeeper let them in.

"Well, I said that if ordinary people like you eat cereal, why shouldn't I?"

Anne failed to smother a laugh.

"What?" said Grace, laughing with Anne without knowing why she was laughing.

Grace and Anne were not ordinary. They were twins, for one

thing. Then they were twin princesses. They took after their mother, who was Queen Luna, having hazel eyes and ash brown hair ... Well, their mother had ash blonde hair, but no matter; their hair still had the colour of ash.

The princesses always woke up at seven o'clock in the morning, except at the start of each season, which happened to be today. Though Anne had used to wake Grace up by climbing the ladder of the bunk bed and shaking her profoundly by the mattress because Grace had failed to wake up any other way, Grace had never failed to wake up since they had started using their own invention – the rooster alarm clock. Since Anne used to wake Grace up, Grace brushed Anne's hair in return; now that Grace didn't need Anne to wake her, she insisted that Anne should repay her hair brushing by some other service, for instance, serving water. Anne pointed out that she had never, ever asked for Grace to attack her hair, and it would be good for everyone if Anne just lived with tangled hair. For one thing, her hair was being practically ripped out, and for another, her hair also broke Grace's brush every morning, and Grace always said it was because she had to buy a brush every day that she had no money although she received pocket money.

A grey sky could be seen through the drawn-back curtains. Anne and Grace had always liked the large windows. Servants pulled out their chairs and poured milk on their cereal before retreating to the wall. Anne and Grace seated themselves.

"You know," said Anne slowly, spreading a napkin on her lap.

"What?" said Grace.

"Today is the first of December," said Anne, grinning, "which means –"

"Oh," said Grace. "Yeah. The Opening for the Festival of Winter." She grimaced.

"Don't you like it that we get to dress in beautiful dresses?" asked Anne. "Don't you like to see the sunrise?"

"Well, we wear beautiful dresses all the time," said Grace, raising her spoon. "And although you fancy decorating yourself very specially, you always look like you always do, since you're too embarrassed."

"Right," said Anne, frowning. "And I hate dancing. I always have to make up lame excuses not to take part in the dance. Maybe this time I'll put on shoes that aren't suitable for dancing."

"Maybe we can accidently step on one another's toes when we're about to join," agreed Grace, sipping milk from her spoon. "The food's really tasty, though, and yeah, I love seeing the sun rise. The dawn is so beautiful."

They were peacefully munching on their cereal when the door suddenly burst open. King Lentris stepped in, putting them out of motion for a moment with surprise.

"Oh," said Anne, breaking into a smile and chomping up another spoonful of cornflakes. "Hey, Dad!"

She lifted her hand as a salute. The door slowly closed behind King Lentris. A servant pulled out his chair which was at the head of the table and poured his milk.

"Why is he like that?" Grace whispered to Anne, never taking her eyes off him as he made his way towards them with an unreadable expression.

"Did you put wet tissues in his shoes again?" asked Anne, looking reproachfully at Grace, puzzled as King Lentris stared at them.

"No."

"Did you put frogs in *his* bed, now?"

"No," Grace replied. "You can stop glaring at me, Anne."

"I wasn't *glaring* at you, I was just –"

"You two!" said King Lentris suddenly, glaring at them as if they had just betrayed him like Brutus. "How could you? I should send you to prison straight away!"

"What are you talking about?" said Anne, gaping at him. The servants shuffled uncomfortably as they stood by the walls.

"So abrupt," murmured Grace behind her.

"Girls, girls, don't try to fool me," said the King, leaning over to speak in a harsh whisper the servants would not be able to hear. "You stole the *queen's ring*, that's what you did, and that's what I'm talking about!"

The twins involuntarily let out a gasp at the same time. Whoever had the queen's ring had the Queen's throne too.

"Who stole it?" asked Grace at last, rather dumbly.

"Who else but you?" he growled.

"Um ... I didn't steal it. Maybe Anne did ..."

Grace earned a little pinch from Anne.

"She isn't quite awake from her sleep yet, I think," said Anne. "But anyway, why do you suggest that the thief is us? It might just be lost. You know we wouldn't steal our mum's ring, right? I mean –"

"Calm down, anyway, Dad," Grace growled. "That isn't a proper way of discussing things, is it?"

"*Are you lecturing me, now?! –*"

Before King Lentris could finish his sentence, the door burst open a second time, surprising him into silence, as if a bucket of cold water had been thrown upon him. Queen Luna stood in the doorway, her hair untidy and her lady-in-waiting Granny by her side, looking anxious. It looked as though Queen Luna had dressed rather hastily.

"Has anyone seen my ring?" she asked in a small, tense voice, in contrast to the noise she had caused in banging the door open. Looking around and seeing that no one moved, she slowly made her way to the table with a hand on her forehead. "I clearly, clearly remember putting it back in the little black box – like I always do! And now, it just disappears, along with the box! Gone! Lost!" She threw up her hands with helplessness, and her expression was blank, as if she just couldn't believe the fact that she had lost the ring. She looked up, perplexed beyond feeling perplexed. "I *lost* it, Lentris. I –"

Queen Luna finally noticed the servants and tried to restrain herself. She drew a shaky breath and put her face into her hands, and Anne thought she heard a sob. King Lentris stirred slightly, as if he wanted to comfort her, but he stood stiffly where he was. The servants pulled out her chair and poured her milk, and they all hastily retreated out of the hall.

"Your daughters have stolen it," he said at last, with a constricted voice that sounded like he was choking back tears. He stared pointedly at the ground with a clenched jaw whenever Queen

Luna looked at him and wouldn't meet her eyes except to snatch glances of her expression when she wasn't looking, bringing it to Anne's attention. Queen Luna looked up, her expression fully expressing her immense relief. She looked weak from the worry that she had just been in seconds ago.

"Was that just another prank of yours, Grace?" she said, grinning. "Goodness, I thought I had really lost it! You can give me the ring back in the afternoon, if you want, since you've reaped a great reaction already."

She sighed with relief and beamed at them, cooling her hot face with her hands.

"I'm afraid we can't."

"Grace," said Anne hastily. "She won't understand you if you talk like that."

Queen Luna, whose ease had vanished, was looking possibly even more vexed than before.

"Mum, I'm sorry for you," said Grace, explaining herself, "but we don't have it. Plus, we didn't steal it."

Everyone became aware of a squeaking noise that occupied the would-be silence. All eyes turned to a maid, who was calmly wiping the windows. The maid noticed that she was the source of the long silence and looked up.

"Oh, hello, sirs," she said eagerly. "I mean, your majesties – I'm new here, pardon me. I hope you are having a good day ..."

Seeing their expressions, she accidently dropped the mop and stooped down to retrieve it. Looking flustered, she dropped into a curtsey and knocked over the bucket of water in the process, blushing profusely. The maid hurriedly mopped up the water while King Lentris reached for the bell. A second later, the housekeeper had come rushing through the door and was now bustling the confused maid out of the hall.

The royal family ate their cereal in stony silence, every one of them shocked and worried and perhaps angry. Finally, King Lentris lay down his spoon, as if he couldn't bear to eat another mouthful.

"Luna, this is a serious problem. If they have the ring, one of them would be Queen ..."

"Your majesty my King, may I speak my opinion?" said Granny quietly.

King Lentris stared at her for a moment, then nodded briefly.

"I can't help but notice," she said, "that it is most unlikely that Her Royal Highnesses Princess Grace and Anne should desire the very ring that should come into their possession in due time, risking everything to steal it from their own mother."

"Grace is the firstborn, and therefore heiress to the crown," said King Lentris. "Perhaps Anne wants to be the heiress instead. Perhaps she wants the queen's ring because she knows, in due time, the ring would be passed on to Grace."

Queen Luna looked shocked that King Lentris should suggest such a thing, while Grace indignantly put her fist into her cereal bowl for Anne's sake.

"So, you mean to accuse me, Dad?" said Anne slowly, while Grace hurriedly mopped up the spilt milk with her napkin. "If you must know, Grace can tell you I was with her the whole time, and you can trust Grace would not lie because she has no reason to cooperate in the plot that would rob her of her rights."

"My King, I assure you that Anne's strong affection for Grace cannot permit such an act," Granny quickly put in, while reaching over to assist Grace.

"But what if Grace's strong affection of Anne prevents her from telling the truth?" said King Lentris, raising his voice. "What if Grace is cooperating in the plot that would rob her of her rights because of this affection?"

"Surely, you have gone too far!" said Grace angrily, tossing away the napkin. "Do you think I'm blind or do you think I'm stupid? For according to what you have said, you are plainly suggesting thus, unless I am also deaf! And I am certain you have been cooped up in your royal duties for too long, or you would have known that Anne has a better conscience and affection than five of you –"

"I should think that is enough," said Queen Luna, putting down her spoon. The others looked at her.

"Luna, even our own daughters should receive the punishment they require," said King Lentris, quickly turning to face her. "A king should not be partial to his own. One of them, or both, should be sent to the prisons."

There was a pause, as if everyone had forgotten to breathe. Then Granny, Anne, and Grace opened their mouths at the same time.

"My King, no one can yet be sure who stole the ring!"

"In case you have forgotten, we're not even of age –"

"And I haven't even finished my breakfast!"

Grace was looking at King Lentris as if he had just suggested she should try some dog food.

"Lentris," said Queen Luna coldly. "I cannot see the reason why you are so sure that our daughters have taken the ring. For all we know, I might have just lost it. Give them time, and they will be able to prove their innocence. You know they have been honest so far, and to talk of punishment is a step too early."

"Honest?" said King Lentris. "For all I know, there was never a day they had not stolen cookies –"

"– Five years ago," finished Anne. "*Five years ago*. Did we steal important or expensive things, like jewelry? – or your royal papers? Even when it was well within our reach we did not do so; we only stole what we would return for mere fun of reaction as a light joke."

"And if you think cookies are the same as rings that make people Queen," added Grace, "if you think jokers are no different from criminals –"

"Every crime starts small," said King Lentris.

In the mid-afternoon, the princesses' mother knocked at their bedroom door.

"Come in," came the reply.

Queen Luna opened the door and stepped inside. Grace was crouched up on the upper bunk bed, while Anne was at her usual spot sitting on the ladder's second step with her arms fitted around the ladder. They were both in their jumpers and trousers.

Queen Luna crossed the room and opened the window to let in the fresh air. The girls waited in what seemed a hushed silence.

The Queen turned around and sat upon the window sill, her arms crossed.

"Well, I saw you weren't at the Opening," she said conversationally. The two exchanged a glance, then nodded.

"Your father looked rather downcast," she continued, peering at their expressions. "And, I also observed, you've both cancelled your most favorite lessons, which today included how to walk on mud without making a trace."

"We've already learnt that," Anne blurted out, "as well as –"

"Of course, I know neither of you stole my ring," said the Queen, as if she knew what the twins were thinking of and finally going to the waited point. "But there is a very strange, very unreasonable law concerning it."

Grace and Anne's face flushed rather indignantly.

"Laws, as you know," continued Queen Luna, "can't really be broken by kings or queens no matter how silly it might be. The law does say the person with the queen's ring becomes Queen, and being so, this matter becomes very serious to all of us."

"That law should be destroyed!" said Grace, punching her pillow into a comfortable shape before squishing it thoroughly again.

"I know it's ... *strange*," said Queen Luna, "that your father keeps insisting you being the ones who stole the queen's ring. Anyhow, I told him to give you *at least* ten days in order to prove your innocence, so Lentris gave you ten days at the *most* – though I find it completely useless, and more so even if you were the ones who have stolen the queen's ring. According to that law, as long as you keep the ring, never minding the method used to take it, one of you *would* become queen when a new king sits on the throne – though queens also can be chucked into jail."

"Thank you," said Anne at last, and Grace grunted, meaning the same thing.

"I do hope you find a way to convince your father into believing the truth that is dancing in front of his face," said Queen Luna. "If you don't ... well, I don't know what will be done, but the idea of chucking young girls into prison without solid proof that they did wrong because they were unable to prove otherwise ... That is absurd. That is really absurd." She sighed. "Really, none of our family is safe now."

"All because of that law," Grace pointed out. "What idiotic weirdo made it?"

"King Thalein is the weirdo," said Anne, peering over her shoulder at Grace. "He made that law to protect the Queen's rights, in the first place, but he probably didn't foresee that someday, it might be used against the Queen."

"Oh," said Grace, frowning. She became silent. Queen Luna and Anne exchanged a look and grinned. Grace caught them in the act and began to look extremely disgruntled.

"I wouldn't mind dying," said Queen Luna suddenly and quickly, the smile flickering on her lips. "For my people, or my family, or for something good, I wouldn't mind."

She hesitated for a moment, then reached for the doorknob and quickly walked out, leaving the girls staring at the spot she had been standing on.

After eating lunch, the girls locked themselves inside their room. Grace made a count-down paper to count the days that were left, while Anne hardly thought that necessary, and Anne got two sheets of scrap paper, though Grace said she didn't think they should write anything down. They were going to hold a two-person meeting to plan what they were going to do.

"As you know, we're going to hold a meeting," said Grace, ticking out 'day one' on the chart she had made. "First, let's talk about how to find the real criminal."

"I think it's kind of funny to state that we're holding a meeting even though you did say 'as you know' in front," said Anne, grinning. Grace frowned.

"That's not the point," she said.

"Okay, sorry," said Anne hastily. "Then you start the meeting officially, if you want."

"There's no need to do *that*, though," Grace muttered, shuffling through the papers even though there was nothing written on it. "Um, let's just talk about who might be the real ... *criminal* ... shall we?"

"Yep," said Anne. "I think it's Dad. I get the feeling that he's just pressing us to the title instead of him. And he seems to be very sure that we stole the ring. Besides –"

"Besides, how could he know the ring was gone even before Mum herself, I was thinking the same thing," said Grace excitedly. "And by the way, he isn't an outstanding actor. He was seriously over-acting."

"Huh, yeah, you should hear his fake-snoring!" said Anne, chuckling. "Oh yeah, you already have, but anyway, please don't interrupt me."

"I get excited when you state the things I was thinking of," said Grace apologetically. "But why would Dad steal the ring? It's no use to him anyway since he's King, unless he stole it to give it to a woman ..."

"In which case his life becomes worthless," said Anne flatly. "It would be the most foolish thing to do."

"Yeah, well, no surprises," said Grace darkly. "He's the descendant of King Thalein, right? The idiotic weirdo who made the idiotic law."

"*Don't say that,*" whispered Anne dramatically with a fake shudder. "What becomes of us?!"

The two looked at each other, then burst out laughing.

"Uh, yeah, I shouldn't say so," Grace admitted, wiping her eyes. "Okay, now, um, what are we going to do next?"

"Let's see what he's going to do," said Anne in a matter-of-fact tone. "Let's wait till midnight because –"

"That's the time most baddies get to work," said Grace. "At least, unauthorized and inexperienced baddies like Dad; they think the middle of the night is somehow the best time that they can be hidden ... Don't forget to sleep."

"But –"

"Or else you're gonna be tired and think like your ancestor Thalein because your head is about to pull on pajamas," said Grace solemnly. "And come to think of it, we might fall asleep in the middle of a desperate chase."

"Yeah, well, *you* might, but *I* –"

"No buts, go to bed," snapped Grace. "Your health is more

important than this. You're young, and to grow you need sleep."

"We're supposed to be the same age, remember?" said Anne. "You sound like some old hag who –"

"Yeah, so I'm *gonna* sleep," said Grace, ignoring Anne's last words. "Duh."

Anne grumbled that Grace had interrupted her yet again. She wasn't good at poking into the conversation at just the 'right time', while Grace got off smoothly most of the time. Despite all this, she did change into her pajamas.

"Pst, Grace, what if you don't wake up?" Anne whispered anxiously as they lay in the bottom bunk bed. "Promise not to yell out or get angry at me or get irritated because you want more sleep when I try to wake you."

"Shut up," Grace murmured.

"You're not supposed to say that!" said Anne, sitting up and banging her head on the top bunk in her indignation. "It's very rude, I don't like it, and you are a *princess* –"

"Yeah, whatever, just sleep, you need it," Grace said yawning, knocking Anne back down with a clumsy gesture, already drifting off, even though it was only afternoon, and surely, she didn't lack sleep. Anne thought it must be a real super power, though that super-natural power came with a mighty inconvenience because Grace also slept when she shouldn't sleep further.

Because of Grace, the princesses slept until finally midnight came with its dark black cloak, casting a shadow on the girls' faces and quietly announcing its arrival by the low gonging of the tower clock. It is a strange thing, but as the princesses were usually so unique, it isn't surprising that, though they were asleep, they somehow knew in their minds that it was exactly midnight. It was time for them to wake and act.

Grace sat up. She bent over and nudged Anne.

"I'm already awake," whispered Anne, putting a finger to her lips, frightening Grace, who had thought she was asleep. The two slid off the bed and changed into some comfortable clothes and shoes. They both put on their backpacks, which both contained different things. They glided towards the door. Anne tried opening it, but the door made an awful, croaking, dying noise.

C-r-e-a-k!

She stopped. Grace disappeared. She reappeared with a small flask of oil. Together they smeared oil on the hinges of the door with a brush, because it would be inconvenient if their hands were smeared with oil. Grace opened the door and rushed out, finding a place to hide. She was shortly after followed by Anne, who had put the oil down by one side then closed the door quietly before joining Grace behind a curtain.

"This hiding place is lousy," whispered Anne, while Grace energetically put her finger to her lips, motioning for Anne to keep quiet. They made their way down the stairs and past the corridor, waiting till the guards patrolled away and moving on before they came back again.

"There he goes," whispered Grace, as they watched a guard move out of sight. They exchanged a glance and sniggered, then moved quickly to the next hiding spot. They were nearly to the staircase that led to the King and Queen's sleeping chambers when they heard voices. Anne peered around the corner to see two guards talking quietly to each other. She hastily shoved Grace behind her when she tried to peer over her.

"– according to Jake, that is," one of them were saying. "I mean, well, I'm not supposed to tell you ..."

"There you go again!" exclaimed the other. "Exactly 'ow many times do you plan to repeat tha' phrase? You *can* tell me; your li'le bro Jakey knows me."

There was silence for quite a while, at which the princesses felt very impatient at the guards, who weren't doing their duty of patrolling their section of the castle and were gossiping but not letting them know the secret which was costing them this obstruction from getting across. Grace was having a silent argument with Anne, who was telling Grace that she should definitely not walk over and tell them for heaven's sake to keep their big fat mouths shut and do their duty as long as they want to keep their jobs.

"See 'ere, if you're gonna tell me, tell me now," said the nosy person, at which their silent argument hastily ended. " 'Else, jus' don't mention it."

"Mind your own business," mouthed Grace.

Jake's brother was silent for a split second, at which Grace and Anne hoped he would be a faithful brother, before he blurted out, "It's about the queen's ring."

Grace and Anne were stunned. Then the nosy person said, "*The* queen's ring?"

"Yeah, like, how many queen's rings are there?" said Jake's brother. "According to Jake, the Queen seems to have lost it."

"Must've been a shock for 'er," said the shocked voice of the nosy person.

"Like you care," mouthed Anne furiously. Grace quietly patted her on the back.

"But you know, I've been wondering," said Jake's brother, who seemed to be enjoying breaking his brother's trust. "The Queen said she remembered putting it in the black box like she always does ... but she also said the box disappeared with it."

"So, you s'pose someone stole it?"

Grace was nearly to her patience's end – she had heard enough and was itching to hurtle around the corner to inform the guards that they had been fired because of their extraordinary incapability to keep their noses to themselves, if only Anne would loosen her painful, vice-like grip on her wrist. Then they heard footsteps coming down from the staircase. Anne released Grace, who immediately clutched at her wrist, testing each one of her precious fingers for broken bones. The guards had become silent and seemed to be hastily patrolling at last.

Grace and Anne heard new voices. Then Grace nudged Anne with big, round eyes.

"It's Dad and his advisor Risephe!" she whispered. "What can it mean?"

They concentrated on listening to what they were saying.

"... may fall asleep during winter," said their father. Clearly, the conversation was at its end, because they spoke no more.

Grace motioned to Anne, and they hastened to follow the King and his advisor, not knowing where they were heading. King Lentris and Advisor Risephe went out into the garden through a door guarded by a guard. Anne and Grace waited for a while, wrapping themselves with cloaks from their backpacks, before stepping out as if they had not been hiding a moment before, as if they had been walking down the same corridor by mere coincidence, and heading to the same garden the King and his advisor were in right now.

Anne beamed at the guard, Grace following her lead.

"Pleasant ... midnight, is it not?" Anne said brightly to the guard while looking out the window into the dark garden, who looked pleased and honored at receiving a direct address from the princess. Anne let her eyes rest on the figures of the King Lentris and his advisor. "Oh, there they are," she said to Grace. "We should join them, by all means!" She turned towards the door, and the guard let them out.

Once out, Grace and Anne shared a smile, then while acting as if to join them, they veered around and let the trees hide them in case the guard was watching them. The men stopped in front of a wooden structure that looked like a gardening shed.

"Ooh," whispered Grace. "The gardener is a very scary old man, he snapped at me when I was just trying to determine what kind of smell a rose has ..."

"I know," Anne whispered back, as they hid behind a rose bush. "I was right beside you that time."

The princesses looked on carefully to see what their dad and his advisor would do, but they only seemed to be talking.

"I can't hear what they're talking about," said Grace, straining her neck as far as she dared. "Can you?"

Anne shook her head. Then the King and his advisor turned around so quickly that Grace lost her balance. Anne quickly lashed out a helpful hand. The men returned the way they had come, much to the girls' disappointment.

After waiting a moment, the girls set after them again. The guard let the King and Advisor Risephe inside. He had a faint trace of wonder on his face, maybe because the princesses had not joined the King's company.

"Let's hope Dad just thinks that guard always looks surprised," whispered Grace anxiously.

They stepped out from behind the rose bushes, carefully smoothing out their cloaks, and came out of the trees again, pretending to be in deep conversation.

"I know!" said Grace, giggling uncharacteristically. "Poor thing, she'll probably be sent to the kitchens after that."

Anne slightly inclined her head as the guard let them in, carrying on their conversation.

"I hope she's not too mortified," she said, "for I think I would have cried."

After they had moved out of earshot from the guard, they instantly fell silent. Hurrying down the corridor and meeting with a rather bewildered young guard, they hastily acted nonchalant, then hid the moment they had the chance to. They caught sight of King Lentris and his advisor disappearing around a corner and waited impatiently for the guard to move away before they rushed to that corner. When they had turned around the corner, they made their way up the staircase where they had first seen the King and his counselor. Crouching down, they saw King Lentris and Advisor Risephe part ways. The King seemed to be heading towards his private library. He opened the door and went in. There was a wall painting by the door, where various scenes were depicted. There was a red dragon spouting fire at the sky in one of the scenes, which Grace vaguely knew to be Cairdew. In the dark corridor, the dragon was only a darker shadow, but it looked more forbidding than in daylight when the redness could be seen vividly.

The girls quietly slipped into the library, hearts pounding. Moonlight was streaming in through the windows. Anne had not realized that tonight was the full moon. They crept carefully, peering over the side of the rows of thick, white bookcases before proceeding. At last they faced the wall – in which bookcases were built in.

"He's not here!" whispered Anne. "We definitely saw him come in, and we definitely checked every row, and unless he's been purposefully hiding from us, we would have seen him ... You don't suppose he is hiding from us, do you?"

Anne looked at Grace, who was looking intently at the bookcase in front of them.

"Grace?" asked Anne uncertainly, she too staring at what Grace was squinting at. "Don't squint, it's bad for your eyes," she added, fishing out a matchbox from her pockets.

Grace struck a match and held it close to the bookcase. The light revealed a small groove in the surface of the bookshelf. Actually, it wasn't a groove at all. It seemed to be a rather deep hole, like a ...

"A keyhole!" said Grace triumphantly, grinning, and dropping the match before stamping on it. "Hairpin, please."

— CHAPTER THREE —

The Underground

Anne plucked a hairpin from her hair and gave it to her sister. Grace inserted the hairpin and picked the lock. Anne grabbed the hairpin and put it back on her hair, while Grace somehow gripped a shelf and pulled the door open. They looked into the pitch blackness, wondering how they were going to make their way in an unfamiliar place without being able to see. Together, they took a step inside and closed the door behind them. Anne struck another match, and they could see that they were at the top of a winding staircase.

"Haven't you got a candle?" asked Grace under her breath, groaning ever so slightly as the match burned out, letting the darkness swallow up all features once again.

"No ..." Anne whispered back. "But I have plenty of matches, so we'll be fine."

Grace silently groaned again.

They made their way down step by step, Grace feeling the wall and Anne clutching her elbow. After a long while, Grace let out a hiss of pain.

"Ouch!"

"What is it?" said Anne, while Grace bent down. Anne struck another match and saw Grace crouching down to rub the toe she had stubbed on a large, wooden door that stood right in front of them. The light died out.

"Where's the keyhole?" said Grace. "Is there a keyhole?"

Anne struck another match and successfully found the keyhole beside the iron knob. She tested the knob, just in case, but like both had expected, it was locked. Anne automatically gave Grace her hairpin since Grace liked to pick the locks.

"Show-off," she teased affectionately.

When they carefully eased open the heavy door, they were delighted as orange torchlight flickered at the walls. Though the torchlight didn't do much, at least they could see in front of them.

"Grace, do you notice that the walls are made of dirt?" whispered Anne.

"Yeah," Grace whispered. "But I rather think we're underground."

Then she quickly tugged at Anne's sleeve to be silent, indicating to where King Lentris was walking ahead of them. Exchanging a glance, they hastened to quietly close the door. Four large wooden carts were propped against the dirt wall.

They followed King Lentris, feeling rather exposed, keeping their distance in case he should see their shadows.

"Aren't there any suitable hiding places?" complained Grace. "Now if Dad happens to turn around, we may pretend to be lost moles, or pretend to sleepwalk, or else you may valiantly take the blame while I graciously hide behind you."

"In the meantime," whispered Anne crossly, "you may be most helpful in keeping quiet."

King Lentris did not look around, not even once. They walked for quite a while. Anne jumped when Grace's stomach rumbled alarmingly loud.

"Sorry," whispered Grace.

At last they reached another large wooden door. King Lentris fumbled for the key, then he slipped inside, closing the door behind him. Grace and Anne exchanged a glance before cautiously easing open the door to following him in.

A faint scent of sweet fruits reached their noses, replacing the musty smell of damp underground. The room they were in seemed to be rather dry.

"Grace," whispered Anne under her breath. "We're in a storeroom."

Grace saw that this was true. Before them were rows of shelves laden with sacks full of fruits and vegetables. There were another two wooden carts here, put to one side.

They closed the door quietly like last time and hid behind the shelves of food.

"Sweet potatoes!" exclaimed Grace suddenly. "Do you think I can eat one? I'm starving."

"Nah, it doesn't look very healthy and it's got sprouts," whispered Anne. "Anyway, it's not cooked."

"You don't need to cook sweet potatoes to eat them," said Grace grumpily. They moved on.

"What about some dried watermelons?" asked Grace a moment later.

"Where?" whispered Anne looking around. She spotted the dried watermelons, looking like some weird, vivid-red jerky, stored in sacks right in front of them. "Wow, I've never eaten dried watermelons before!"

"And there's loads of raisins," whispered Grace, "as well as dried oranges – why is everything dry here?"

"Because if they're dry, they're easier to preserve," Anne whispered back, while Grace felt thankful that she didn't roll her eyes at her. "I wonder what this is all for."

"Perhaps this is where all the food for the palace horses come from," said Grace. "Why aren't those carrots and turnips dry?"

"Maybe they're fresh from the patches and don't have to be stored long," said Anne. "But you know, it seems rather rich even for the King's horses, when they can eat stuff like hay."

The next row was full of oats, wheat, and barley, and next to them were great amounts of hay.

"Well, here's the hay," whispered Grace. "Maybe the dried fruits we saw are just special treats. What an awful lot of treats. But ... yeah," she said, seeing Anne's expression. "I don't see why Dad's here if it's only that."

"Don't you feel a breeze?" whispered Grace suddenly.

"Yeah," said Anne. "I do."

King Lentris reached another winding staircase. A slight, cold breeze seemed to be wafting down from the staircase. Grace and Anne followed him up, Anne wrapping her cloak tightly around herself. The staircase became narrower as they went higher. Then they were out in the fresh air.

"What on earth ...?" whispered Grace. "We're on top of a tree!"

"And my goodness," said Anne, her eyes wide. "It is snowing!"

"Snowing?" said Grace, looking around to see that the branches of their tree were covered with snow. "Golly, you're right ... You know it's very unfair that when wanted snow last winter, we had none, but this winter, when we're too busy to play, we have to take care not to leave any traces or crunching sounds as we secretively follow Dad."

"Come on," said Anne, who had been peering down from the branches and had spotted where King Lentris was walking away.

The moon was still up in the sky, and the sky was slightly brighter than it had been in the garden. The moonlight washed over the white snow and snowflakes lazily drifted down. Anne and Grace slid down the tree, which turned out to be a big oak tree. Anne slid her backpack slowly down her shoulder. She opened her bag and handed Grace a pair of thin, see-through gloves that they themselves had designed. These gloves kept their hands warm but were so light and thin it was like nothing was on their hands.

"Keep your hands warm, dearest sister," said Anne, "though I only have one sister, so you have no competitor anyway."

"Wow, you're great!" said Grace.

"I always am!" joked Anne, putting hers on. Grace jabbed her. Anne jabbed her back. Grace chucked some snow in her face. Anne chucked more snow in her face. Grace chucked even more snow in her face. Anne decided to stop.

Grace blew warm breath on her numb fingers and hurriedly put the gloves on.

"Where's Dad?" she said suddenly. Anne looked around. The trees blocked their view, and the King was nowhere in sight.

"He was going that way, I think," said Anne, pointing to the direction she saw him going. "His footprints must be somewhere."

They searched for his footprints in the moderate layer of snow.

"It must have started snowing while we were underground," muttered Grace to herself. "What time is it anyway?"

"What?" said Anne.

"Nothing," said Grace. "Is this it?"

Anne hurried over to look at what Grace had found.

"It seems to be," said Anne. "It's headed the direction I saw him go. Quick, before we lose him!"

They made their way carefully through the trees, using the skills of leaving no print in the mud to leave no print in the snow. Once or twice one of them made a crunching noise, at which both winced in case King Lentris was hopefully in earshot, which was quite a contradiction. The trees grew thicker, and the snow underneath their feet grew thinner. Finally, the snow had grown so thin that they could no longer see any footprints.

"Where did he go?" asked Anne. Grace gave no answer. Instead, she sprinted off. Anne couldn't call after her in case King Lentris should hear. She tried to follow, but she didn't know where Grace had gone to and the trees were still growing thicker.

Grace realized that she had left Anne behind. She looked behind her. Trees all around her blocked her view. She ventured further, hoping the direction she remembered was correct. She heard footsteps and quickly crouched down. Grace couldn't see where King Lentris was, but clearly it was his footsteps, for he was also murmuring to himself in a low voice.

"... must be enough, it must be worth it. They will understand ... I have to take hold of it ..."

It seemed as if he was convincing himself about something Grace didn't quite get. She understood that he must be talking about the queen's ring, but what was 'worth it'? As Anne said, the thought that he would give it away to some other woman was plausible, plausible if only it didn't thrust his life into danger. Who would do such a foolish thing? But then if not so, there would be no reason for him to steal the ring. It was an incontrovertible fact that he had stolen the ring, owing to his strange behavior and uncanny knowledge. Or was it? ... No, it was definitely him – if she was to doubt even the basic belief on which they had based their acts, there would be nothing to believe. But she wouldn't have ever dreamed that her dad would do such a thing, while she drooled in her sweet sleep before she had been surprised at breakfast time. It was unbelievable, how such a kind and loving dad could just turn 180 degrees in a day's time? ... Of course, it would be his outward behavior that was changed in a day's difference. He wouldn't have suddenly made up his mind that morning to steal a ring and make a colossal drama out of it. Anyway, if he supposed *they* understood him, he was terribly mistaken; it was beyond Grace to understand him.

As his footsteps faded away, Grace jumped to her feet. She had to get to Anne. What did he mean, 'have to take hold'? Have to take hold of what? She had found King Lentris, and now she just had to find Anne to let her know and follow him again. Then a thorn bush blocked her way. There had been no thorn bush ... She hadn't passed this way before. Grace was forced to turn around. The prospect of getting lost in these unfamiliar woods all alone was frightening, and she began to run.

Remembering how she had left Anne alone, she hoped Anne wasn't lost like herself. She stopped to catch her breath. Calming down, she realized there was nothing to panic about. She cupped her hands to her mouth and hooted loudly. Listening carefully if Anne would answer, she became aware of feet snapping twigs and crumpling fallen leaves. Before she could react, Anne barreled into her and knocked her down.

"Sorry," gasped Anne, helping her back up. "Where have you been?"

"I met with Dad," said Grace, gasping herself at the impact on her ribs. As Anne's eyes grew round with horror, she added hastily, "I mean I found him – not that he found me."

"Okay," said Anne, looking relieved.

"It's a shame I lost my way ... I don't know where he is anymore," Grace continued. "Listen, when I heard his footsteps, I crouched down to hide myself. He was kind of muttering to himself, and he said something like, 'It must be worth it, they will understand' and 'I have to take hold of it' –"

"Take hold of what?" said Anne, not looking very relieved.

"I don't know, that's all I heard," said Grace impatiently. "I realized that I had left you, and I tried to go back the way I came but I got lost ... Do you have any idea what direction we came from?"

"Um ..." said Anne nervously, and Grace's heart sank. "I'm not sure," she admitted reluctantly because she was usually good at finding the way back. "But we might have come from there."

She pointed in the direction she had come from.

"What about Dad?" Grace said as Anne led the way. "What

are we supposed to do, now we've lost him? We didn't really have any other plan."

"Our plan right now," Anne replied, "is to get ourselves unlost."

The trees began to grow thinner, and Grace began to hope they had found their way back, but Anne's expression was dark.

"I think we're lost," she mumbled. "I've never come this way before."

They reached an opening, and Grace gladly stepped out from the trees. Anne looked rather gloomy.

"Anne, it's okay," said Grace. "At least we're not stuck in those trees now."

"But we're still lost," Anne pointed out.

"Perhaps we could ask?" suggested Grace. Anne turned to look at where Grace was gesturing to and saw what looked like a small, ramshackle cottage and a rickety stable. Around the cottage and the stable was a snow-covered vegetable patch that could be identified because of its orderly planted shoots, and around the vegetable patch was a rickety fence with a rickety gate.

"I don't think anyone has lived there for at least a couple of years," said Anne doubtfully.

"How come the vegetable patch is so well tended, then?" said Grace, pulling Anne along with her.

"Maybe someone does tend those carrots," said Anne as they drew closer enough to know. "But it doesn't necessarily mean that person lives in this dangerous-looking house."

Just then, they heard a neighing noise coming from the stables.

"Well, surely the person who *once lived* ... or is *still living* in this cottage wouldn't have abandoned a horse," said Grace, beaming.

"It would be cruel to let a horse starve, but anyway, since the horse we have heard has not starved to death and has the energy to neigh, someone has lived here in less than one week."

"Or less than one month, if they stacked enough hay," Anne said. "Same as the carrots. We can't be sure."

Grace knocked on the door of the cottage. There was no answer. Anne cautiously turned the knob. They opened the door.

"Anyone here?" called Anne. Again, there was no answer. They stepped inside.

"Look at these horse hoofprints!" said Grace, pointing to the floor where traces of hoofprints could be seen, caked with dirt. Anne looked at it curiously. Grace grinned. Anne always liked to explore. She left Grace and disappeared into some room. Grace looked up at the uncertain ceiling, thinking how they should find their way now it was certain there was no one to ask. Anne seemed to be muttering something in that room. Just then, there was a thump, and dust poured down from the ceiling.

"Let's get out of here," called Grace. "Maybe this place is finally about to collapse."

Grace walked to the direction Anne had disappeared and found a door. She opened the door and went inside. What surprised her was that this room seemed to be perfectly stable. There were still hoofprints upon the floor, though Grace couldn't imagine why. She noticed some scrawl on one corner of the wall and crouched down to read it.

"Mmm," she said, squinting at the tiny scrawl. " 'What is the title of Didlit Didlum's first tale?' Tulp, of course, this is too easy! Who wrote that question?!"

Just as Grace was about to stand up and leave, the floor gave a jolt and began to descend. Grace froze. Then she tried to jump back up, but the walls were too high. When the floor had finally stopped descending, she found herself looking into the darkness, a staircase leading deeper down. A faint, regular thumping noise could be heard. She hesitated, then called out, "Anne?"

She stepped forward and began to descend the steps. The stone steps were rather slippery. Suddenly, she lost her footing and went tumbling down the slippery steps, not daring to scream. She landed with a big thump on a cold wet floor.

"Hi," said a voice. Grace yelled aloud with fright before she realized it was Anne. Anne looked rather scared.

"We have to go back up," she said, trying to lift Grace to her feet. "Come on, before it closes again."

A little winded by her fall, Grace struggled to get up and ran alongside Anne up the staircase. Her eyes had not adjusted to the sudden darkness. On second thought, hearing Anne stumble beside her, it seemed like there was not the smallest light to adjust on. The opening had closed. Anne clutched at Grace.

"Where's your matches?" asked Grace, feeling her way to a wall. "What's the matter with you – why are you so fretful?"

"Didn't you read the question?"

"I did."

"Well," said Anne, striking a match. "What do you think? This thumping noise? Underground tunnels?"

"Underground tunnels?" Grace repeated. "I don't know where this place is or anything, but I'm rather certain this tunnel ... if it is a tunnel, does not relate to the other. I knew Dad must have a secret tunnel of his own to go in and out of the castle – who wouldn't want a bit of privacy?"

"You know the story of Tulp, right?" asked Anne.

"Of course!" said Grace. "Who doesn't? ... Well, I may have forgotten a bit, but I knew the title."

"The thing is," said Anne hurriedly, "don't you think ... don't you think all the food stored there was for some creatures or one big creature that was supposed to be fed in secret? Why else would the store be underground, or, a part of the secret tunnel of Dad's private use, like you said?"

"You mean – you mean to say ..." stammered Grace.

"Yes!" said Anne, striking another match with trembling hands. "But you do know of the legends where Tulp is said to be like Cairdew? Fierce, and terrible?!"

"We have to get out of here!" cried Grace, realizing the thumping noise had grown significantly bigger. "Does it know where we are?"

"I suppose it would be able to smell very well," said Anne shivering. "And anyway, I think it was close enough to hear you yell."

Just then, something caught Grace's eye and made her look beyond Anne. In the dim light of the match, she made out a scrawl on the wall very like the one that had led her here.

"There!" she said, and Anne jumped. Realizing what Grace was talking about, Anne struck a match and held it close to the writing.

" 'What is greater than the earth and everything in it?' " she muttered underneath her breath.

"What?" said Grace, despairing. "Greater than the earth and everything in it?"

She looked at Anne, who was reading the riddle again and again in a completely nonplussed expression.

"Um, diamonds?" ventured Grace. "Wait, that's in the earth; it can't be greater than itself ..."

"Space?" said Anne hopefully. "A galaxy? Everything?"

"Nothing?" said Grace. For the moment, her mind seemed to be as blank as her sight.

"Hope?" said Anne desperately. Grace thought that was a welcome idea, when everything seemed hopeless right now. Then her jaw dropped. She had seen the glow of fire, somewhere in the dark depths of the tunnel.

"Silence!" squeaked Anne. "Ambition! Whatever!"

"Friendship!" bellowed Grace. "Memories! Mercy!"

"Love!" said Anne. "Um, time! – woah!"

The floor had descended down to them again. Then Grace gasped, saying, "Oh my goodness ..."

Anne whirled around. She found herself staring into two glowing, yellow eyes.

— CHAPTER FOUR —

An Unexpected Twist

Anne stumbled as the dark shape of the dragon approached. It was watching her.

"Quick, quick," she murmured, clutching Grace, who was frozen on the spot. Grace tore her eyes from staring at the dragon and looked at Anne. They ran onto the floor that would bring them back up.

"Why isn't this going up?!" exclaimed Grace. Her mind was blanking out once again. "For heaven's sake!"

"Come on, I'll give you a boost-up," said Anne, positioning herself. "See if you can reach the ledge. Go onto my shoulders."

Grace stepped onto Anne's knees then onto her shoulders. Anne stood up, and Grace tried to reach for the ledge.

"I ... can't ... reach it," gasped Grace, trying to stretch herself beyond her limit. The ledge was far beyond her reach. "What now?!"

"I'll let you go higher," said Anne. She stretched out her arms, and taking a deep breath, Grace stepped onto Anne's shaking hands. She pushed up her hands. The ledge was still a palm length higher.

"Brace yourself," she said, and she jumped from Anne's hands. She just managed to cling on the ledge by the tip of her fingers, but the next moment fell back to the ground along with Anne.

"Quickly!" cried Anne, grabbing Grace up. Grace ran back up onto Anne's hands. Jumping again, Grace's hands slipped, and Anne bit her lip as Grace landed on her palms.

"I can't reach it!" Grace yelped. "I hope being eaten alive won't be too painful!"

"Try to breathe more slowly, you're breathing too fast," Anne exclaimed. Then Grace's hands finally clamped around the ledge. Anne had stumbled back, but panting, she quickly returned to sustain Grace's feet so she could clamber up, jumping up and down to reach her.

"Have you got a rope?" yelled Grace from above. Anne rummaged her backpack and tossed one end of the rope to Grace. Grace peered around, but there was nothing she could tie the rope to. She bound the rope around her hands and positioned herself. "Come on up, quickly!"

Anne grabbed the rope and began to climb frantically. In her haste, she unluckily got tangled. She eased herself free and climbed up again.

"I wasn't good at rope-climbing," she wheezed, clinging onto the rope with burning hands. Her face was shining red with effort, and the sweat was making her palms slippery.

"QUICK, ANNE!" shouted Grace, all of a sudden starting to pull up the rope that Anne was clinging to with brute force. "Oh no, it breathes fire – now how are we going to escape? IT HAS WINGS!"

"Of course, a dragon has wings," panted Anne feverishly. She was nearly at the top. "But once we're out, it can't follow us ... according to Didlum, it's tied down –"

"It's ... it's right behind you," croaked Grace, shaking. Anne looked around. The dragon was looking into her eyes. Strangely, she began to feel calm as the eyes bore into her. Then she remembered what situation she was in. Taking a deep breath, Grace was stretching out her hand to her. Anne swallowed and inched her hand towards Grace, not daring to let go of the rope. When their fingertips were about to touch, orange light suddenly lit up so brightly that Grace couldn't see anything else, and she gritted her teeth because of the heat, smoke and pressure. She closed her eyes tight.

All was quiet, and the smoke grew sparse. Grace coughed and wiped her stinging eyes. She was very surprised to see that she wasn't holding Anne's hand. Instead, she was holding a piece of charred rope. She dropped it. What had happened? Most of all, where was Anne? Carefully, Grace lowered herself down the ledge until she was clinging on with her fingertips again, and then she jumped down, stumbling to the ground.

"Anne?" she called, but only her echo came back to her. The dragon must have taken her, but how did it take her away so quickly? It couldn't have teleported, or anything like that. Then had she been knocked unconscious? For it seemed that it was, at most, only ten seconds before she opened her eyes.

Where was Anne? Grace felt guilty. She regretted that she hadn't sent Anne up first. She regretted panicking, regretted telling Anne the dragon was right behind her, since that made her look back with the time she ought to have been climbing. She regretted yelling so loud in the first place, though she knew not doing so would have hardly changed anything. She didn't have a clue about what she was to do next. No exact clue, at least. She knew that she had to rescue Anne, and that she's somewhere in this cave kind of place, before that dragon realized it was hungry. Grace sat down in despair. Then she stood up again, partly because there was a warm puddle and mostly because she thought every minute, every second counted. For a moment, she thought she could hear the faint echo of a wail. She hurried her steps, trying to reign her imagination from running ahead. She didn't want to lose Anne, who had been to her the closest friend, the dearest sister, in just a single, unsatisfactory bite of a stupid dragon.

"YOU NINCOMPOOP, YOU OUGHT TO CONSIDER HOW MANY VENGEFUL RELATIVES YOUR VICTIM HAS!" Grace yelled, as if the dragon would be able to hear her if she shouted loud enough. "And to kindly inform you, ANNE HAS A HUNDRED OF THEM SINCE *I'M* WORTH A HUNDRED! Now you know that next time you shouldn't even *think* of eating a sister of Grace, and PITY THERE WON'T BE ANY NEXT TIME WHEN I'M DONE WITH YOU!"

She clutched her throat, which had grown hoarse, and punched the air in revenge. Then she stopped and let out a sob, beginning to feel the emptiness of what had really happened to her.

The cave grew darker, if it was even possible to become any more darker than it already was. Anne had taken all her matchsticks with her, and therefore Grace had to stick to the wall and feel her way along. She didn't know how much time passed – she couldn't, since there was no way to know. She hoped she was going the right way, that there was no other way, because she had no way to know if the tunnel split into two since she was sticking to one side. Then, an orange light lit the atmosphere, lighting up Grace's path and showing her a bend ahead of her. Grace suddenly began to run to the corner, where the light was coming from; she wished Anne was waiting alive and unharmed on the other side – but a split second later, she had been flung back with such a force that she was knocked unconscious again.

King Lentris looked up. A woman stood before him, her face covered by a veil.

"Where is the ring?" she asked.

The King reached into his pocket and brought out the small, black box that held the ring. The woman glanced at it, then looked back at King Lentris.

"We have a deal to make," said King Lentris. "You have brought the lamp, have you not?"

"Of course," said the woman, reaching into her cloak. She pulled out the golden lamp, holding it with both her hands. The lamp had rusted on some parts, and a jewel was missing from its lid.

"Hand me the lamp first," said King Lentris, "Then I will hand you the ring."

"No," said the woman. "*You* will first hand me the ring."

They glared at each other in silence for a while. The woman suddenly moved forward and made to grab the ring, but King Lentris reached out and lifted the woman's veil. With a yelp, she stumbled back and retreated to a wall, but not before he had seen her face.

"Noctren Hortmon?" he said. The woman froze. Then she slowly pulled off her veil, breathing heavily. They both looked down at the ring, then looked back at each other.

"Where have you been, all these days?" asked King Lentris, a shadow of a smile flickering around the corners of his mouth. "We thought you left because –"

"I left because no one wanted me here," said Noctren quickly. "Even my parents loved her more than me, when I'm supposed to be their daughter!"

"What do you mean?" said King Lentris. "Luna loved you, and so did your parents –"

"She wasn't their daughter!" said Noctren. "They only took her because they had no children of their own – but I, their only daughter, was second to her in affection as well as age or anything else!"

"She's from the Hortmon family," said the King, "and if she wasn't –"

"How would you feel if I told you she is descended from Feridan?" said Noctren. "Is that easier to believe than my word?"

"No, I didn't mean that."

"I thought you were different," she continued. "I thought you cared, while Luna was indulged in the attention everyone gave her because she was so sweet and beautiful, talented and kind-hearted – of course, I was always her shadow whom no one noticed. But you became my only friend."

King Lentris could not answer, only to look on her with sympathy.

"But then," said Noctren, her voice becoming rather shrill, "You left me too – I had so foolishly mistaken you! You *used* me to get closer to my dear sister, and you abandoned me the moment I had fulfilled my use to you! You are foul and conceited and *vile*, I don't know why I ever thought any good of you – You don't deserve her ..."

She broke off sobbing.

"But I knew," she said, restraining herself. "I had to act. There was a time I thought Luna was dear to me, but now I would take her place, since she took mine. After all, you seem to have the habit of thinking the people around you are mere as tools to get to your prize, don't you? Surely this practice isn't too unfamiliar for you ... But now you have lost everything. *Everything*, like I once had."

She drew out a dagger from her belt, and King Lentris's eyes grew wide with surprise.

The woman fingered the ring half-heartedly and walked away. The lamp dropped from her fingers to the floor with a dull clatter, and for a moment there was a whiff of green smoke.

Grace woke up. Where was she? She couldn't breathe. She burst out from under a pile of loose gravel and dirt. She looked around her and could see nothing. Then she remembered why she was there, and her mind whirled.

"Anne!" she said aloud. Then she coughed and hacked.

Grace stepped out of the pile of dirt. It was too dark to see. She brushed the soil from her clothes. Her hand brushed upon something lumpy in her pockets. She pulled out a squished matchbox and two candlesticks. She couldn't believe her luck. She opened the matchbox and felt inside. There were four matchsticks in total, but one was broken. She struck a match and lit one candle. She realized that what she thought to be a candle was actually red sealing wax. She hoped it would work just as fine.

Grace quickly rummaged her backpack and found a jar of biscuits. Grimacing, she filled her gloves with the biscuits and knotted up the cuff. Shaking the crumbs out of the jar, she stuck the sealing wax to the bottom, making a makeshift lantern by attaching a handle from a bit of the rope Anne had given her.

From a certain point, the stone tunnel turned into a dirt tunnel. She could now see the dragon Tulp's footprints in the soil. Again, there was an orange glow, but this time very faint, from somewhere up the tunnel. Then there was a low, rumbling noise, like the thunder after a lightning strikes from far off. Suddenly, the tunnel shook. Loose pebbles and rock showered down on Grace as she dodged clumps of earth. She covered her head and began to run. Behind her, the tunnel was swallowed up as the ceiling caved in, and the small flame of the sealing wax danced dangerously inside the lantern. She had no time to look back, only to hear the threatening sound of rumbling. The ground under her was shaking, and she twisted her ankle. Though she bit her lip because of the pain, she couldn't stop, and destruction seemed dangerously near. Taking deep gulps of air, Grace ran still faster.

A huge clump of soil and gravel crashed to the ground, blocking

Grace's way to safety, if there was any. She hoped Anne wasn't in so much danger – though that could hardly be possible, seeing that she was kidnapped by a dragon. In desperation, Grace punched and kicked at the clump, only earning another graze and a sore foot. She couldn't squeeze through the tiny gap between the clump and the side of the tunnel. Then she gave a mighty leap. She managed to clamber over the rough clump just in time, as the earth covered up where she had been a few seconds ago.

Again, much tired out by now, Grace ran. But the tired legs were slowly growing stiffer. Holding the precious lantern in her hands, Grace thought she could see a point where the earth tunnel turned to stone again. Hoping she was right, unable to run any longer, she flung herself onto the hard floor. The last of the soil tunnel came crashing down and the earth tumbled into the stone tunnel, trapping Grace's leg. She lost hold of the lantern. The light went out, and she was left in total darkness. There she lay in a panting heap, as sleep crept stealthily over her. She woke up in a sudden. Grace saw her trapped leg. It was caught somewhere around the ankles. She struggled to pull it out, yanking it, hopping from it, squirming, and lots of ways. The leg came free, causing Grace to tumble backwards. She sat down, massaging her bruised ankle. It seemed impossible to catch up with Tulp now.

"I hope Anne is safe," she said aloud without energy left even to cry. Her mind was growing foggy.

The sun was rising. The Queen woke up in her bed. She yawned, and then peered around her. King Lentris wasn't there. She got up and walked up to the door. She opened the door and peered out, and seeing no one but the eager maid, this time sweeping up the floors, she closed the door. She quickly got dressed and went about, accompanied by her lady-in-waiting. Neither the King nor Grace nor Anne were to be seen. She expected them to be eating breakfast by now and entered the breakfast hall, but they weren't there. The servants pulled out her chair as usual, so the Queen sat down without really meaning to. She held her spoon loosely in her hand with a brooding expression, poking at the soggy cereal, then laid it back down. After a while, she rose and returned to her chambers. She spotted a note beside the mirror.

"What's this?" she thought aloud as she picked it up. She began to read.

Dear Luna,

Good morning!

I suppose you slept well? I am very sorry I had to go out early without saying goodbye to you. I probably won't be back for breakfast. I had an important bargain to deal with, so I went out as early as possible.

I'll return as soon as I can.

Maybe I will be able to explain all this to you when I get back.

Lentris

The handwriting grew crude as the letter went on, as if Lentris had hastily scribbled it in the end, and by the way he had written his name, Luna could hardly identify it as L-e-n-t-r-i-s or as his elaborate handwriting. The last sentence in the letter was all blotched, and the paper was stiff, like he had written it in the rain, or else had wept on it.

The Queen sat down on the bed, examining the blotches.

"A bargain ...?"

A woman in a hooded cloak walked into where the King lay unconscious in his own pool of blood. She muttered a spell, and the King disappeared, as well as the stains on the floor. She took the lamp from the floor and looked around. Then, she too disappeared in a swirl of petals.

— CHAPTER FIVE —

Lilian's Daughter

Queen Luna recalled the queer things King Lentris had done. He had behaved so unlike himself, when he was usually so gentle and good-natured, and slow to accuse someone. He had blamed their loving daughters, who wouldn't have thought of stealing anything. He was the first to know that the ring had been stolen. He had gone early, the day after the ring had been lost – or more likely stolen, to deal with some bargain. Out of anxiety, the Queen stood up again. If what she was thinking was true ... But no. King Lentris might have changed, but no one could turn suddenly so foolish as to bargain for something with their own life. She must stop him. But where was he? If the ring had been already dealt, what could possibly be done? It would be too late; everything would be too late. She walked out of the room, hesitantly knocked, then opened the door to her daughters' room. She found it empty.

"They've gone somewhere too," she thought. Seeing the bottom bunk bed unmade, she put on a motherly frown and despite herself moved forward to make it herself. Then she tripped over a flask of translucent liquid, upsetting it completely with her unintentionally well-aimed kick. Realizing the liquid that was soaking into the carpeted floor was in fact oil, the Queen groaned and was about to relapse into a deeper frown when she noticed the spills that she had just made were not the only ones. Drops of oil clung to the door hinges, while on the floor below was a dark stain, obviously resulted from the same cause the hinges were oiled from. Her face lost its frown. She put one hand on her hip and one below her chin, pursing her lips with another brooding expression.

Grace stood up and tested her ankle. It was fine. She felt around and found the lantern. The sealing wax had been broken off from the bottom of the lantern and lay a few centimeters away. Stowing the lantern and the stubby sealing wax, she started running again, touching the wall now and then to check her course. She didn't stop until she was so exhausted that she felt she couldn't go one step more.

"The dragon certainly had no sleep," she thought absentmindedly. She felt empty. 'Empty' was a weak word for the hunger she felt; it seemed as if she hadn't eaten for a day, which was probably more or less the truth. She hadn't eaten anything from the time she and Anne ate lunch, before sleeping till midnight to follow the King. She got out the gloves and untied the knots to munch on the biscuits. The biscuits were hard and dry, but she wolfed them down, not caring.

Grace could hear the echo of a door sliding open and shutting. She hurried to the place the sound had come from. As she expected, she came to a stop at a door. Striking the second match and hurriedly relighting the lantern, she looked for a keyhole. There wasn't one. She tried to slide it open, but it wouldn't budge. Then, she caught sight of a carved letter, 'o'. She walked up and held the dim lantern close to it. There was a 'w' right next to it.

"Ow," read Grace. It seemed strange. She blew on it, and dust rose from the surface of the door, covering Grace. Sneezing and spluttering, Grace waved away the dust. She stopped waving the air and stared at the 'Ow' word. It had turned into a 'How'. She began to wipe away the dust that had rested on the door's surface. She could make out a sentence: 'How many triangles are in this shape?' Below there was a shape carved in the door. 'Only three chances,' it added.

It looked like two wonky triangles, interlaced to make a third triangle between them.

"Why, there are three triangles," said Grace.

A rock fell from the ceiling so quickly and suddenly that Grace barely avoided it.

'Wrong! Two chances left,' read the door.

"Then two, maybe?"

'Wrong! One chance left,' read the door.

"What?!" roared Grace. She looked at the strange shape carefully. She pressed her nose on the door to look more closely. The closer she looked, the bigger and wonkier the lines became. "It's too wonky to be called a triangle," said Grace cautiously, looking out for any loose rocks that might fall on her. She dreaded to think what might happen if she was wrong. "It has no triangles." Just as it was said, the big door slid open. Grace passed through, thinking it was a very queer riddle to put on such a door.

Grace realized that this side of the tunnel was much brighter than the other side of the door. In order to preserve the little bit of sealing wax that was left, she reached to put out the light, but it sputtered out of its own accord. She took a step and froze. The little 'pat' sound echoed all over. She drew back and began more carefully. Concentrating on every step, she nearly crept right into the dragon. Grace was amazed by the quietness of the big, heavy, dragon. The dragon made nearly no noise. It crept carefully, one foot at a time. Grace wondered why the dragon had been so loud back then by the entrance, with its thumping footsteps and fire breath. Much smaller but faster, Grace silently crept past the dragon's swishing tail, by the way nearly getting swished away by it and barely missing a spike. She spotted a figure hunched upon the dragon's back. Grace quietly let out a sigh of relief to find that it was Anne, and that she was still in one whole piece. But why was her hand dangling lifelessly upon the dragon's scales? After a moment's panic, Grace realized Anne was sleeping. She was sleeping so peacefully!

"What on earth is she doing there, SLEEPING PEACEFULLY when I was worried sick of her and came *all* this way?!" Grace bellowed.

The dragon made no notice, because she had shouted this in her head.

Grace made up her mind to get on to the dragon's back, next to Anne. She would silently wake her up and together they would creep away, unknown to the dragon. She hopped onto the huge leg of Tulp and quickly clambered up, using the cracks in the scales as handholds and footholds. It didn't seem to know; was it because Grace was too small and light for its hard, scaly leg to feel? She reached its belly and hung tightly onto it as the body rippled at each step. She nearly lost hold. Biting her lips with the effort, she heaved herself up ... and finally onto the dragon's back. Panting, she crawled over and nudged Anne.

"What is the matte-b!" Anne mumbled, and got Grace's fist shoved roughly in her mouth. Anne rose up to a sitting position and lifted one heavy eyelid to see who it was. She would have screamed with joy if Grace had not luckily still been putting her fist in Anne's mouth. Anne bit the fist, instead. Grace yanked her fist from Anne's mouth. She would have shoved Anne, but she was afraid Anne would yelp. She stabbed her index finger viciously towards the dragon's head, meaning they were in trouble.

"Oh," mouthed Anne. She began to climb to the dragon's head. "Tulp!" she said ever so slightly, but the word echoed so dreadfully much. Grace was horrified. The dragon stopped going. Slowly, it turned its head. It couldn't see Anne, who was *on* its head.

Bracing herself, Grace slid down the dragon's neck with admirable courage to reach Anne and was about to grab her, but Anne nimbly jumped to the ground and landed softly. The dragon grunted and narrowed its eyes to see Anne. Just then, Grace slid down from the dragon's head and landed next to Anne. Her frustration made her braver than she would have been, and though she doubted Tulp would listen, though she believed he might grunt one moment then swallow her the next, she wanted at least a chance to speak before she was to be eaten alongside Anne. After all, her plan of slipping away secretly had been ruined by Anne's strange behavior.

"Don't eat me," began Grace. "Let's talk. Why did you kidnap Anne? Where are you taking her? Why haven't you eaten her yet ..."

The dragon gave a loud grunt.

"No, I'm speaking right now," snapped Grace. "Why –"

She was interrupted by another grunt.

"Hey, stop doing that!" she said. "You should at least give me a chance to speak before you –"

She was interrupted again when the dragon made some strange, sniffing noises and pawed the ground, grunting again and again.

"Grace, I found out that he wanted to help us," said Anne rather cautiously.

"What? He – who?"

"He's not dangerous," stammered Anne. "I'm sorry – I was worried about you, but Tulp reckoned you'd be terrified if he came back for you, and that you'd follow anyway, catching up courage on your way – which you did, though I'm equally sorry and I haven't done anything good ... I'm *really* sorry! I know how much you'd have worried ..."

"What? Really? Aw man! Hey!" said Grace indignantly, knocking Anne over, thinking of how she had run with the desperation and hope that Anne might still be alive. She felt slightly hurt, too, that Anne hadn't known how worried she had been. Tulp seemed to wince at the echo. "You owe me an apology," she said to Anne, and, turning to Tulp she said, "You too!"

Anne said she was very sorry, and Tulp nodded his head. Grace relented. Tulp bent down, and they clambered back on.

"Where's it taking us?" asked Grace.

"To his cave," answered Anne.

"What do you mean?" said Grace. "Er, this *is* its cave."

"Not quite. He's got another place, his usual place, not here. Its ceiling is higher, and it has an opening where the sunlight ... or moonlight floods in," said Anne. The tunnel grew brighter, and now Grace could clearly see Anne's face. It was strange how precious the sight seemed after for a long time she thought Anne might be dead.

Finally, they arrived.

"He's going to need our help first, to help us," said Anne. "He's tied with an invisible rope. We'll have to set him free. After he helps us, he's going to fly back to his real home."

"How do you know all this?" asked Grace.

"Some parts I read in the fairytale book in our bedroom, some parts from history and geography, some you and I heard from Dad –"

"What, you remembered them?" interrupted Grace.

"Yeah, didn't you?" asked Anne. "Anyway, the other parts, Tulp told me, and it all fits smoothly."

"But then, do you mean it's chained?" said Grace, looking around to see if there were any chains she had missed. "Who chained it, with what reason? How is it a nice dragon?" Grace folded her arms and raised one eyebrow in the classical skeptic gesture.

"I'd better tell you his whole story," said Anne, smiling, partly because she liked telling stories, partly because she liked telling them to Grace, and mostly because of Grace's posture. "First let's get off Tulp. He might fall asleep on top of us."

The two girls jumped off the dragon as he lay down to sleep. Anne took a very dramatical, deep breath and paused to see the effects, but it wasn't much, so she gave up with a little sigh and plainly started to speak.

"Tulp lived in a place which I'm not sure is on our maps. It must be very far away, anyhow. He lived in this place with a waterfall, in a paradise, with willow trees, streams, flowers, grass –"

"It doesn't sound much different from our good old Tertalin," said Grace. "What's so paradise-like about it?"

"There were also animals like windlets and brownies."

"What's the point of living there if they have no household labors to work out?" said Grace with a grin, perhaps thinking the brownies would only be too happy to serve her water anytime. "I mean, it would be really useful for our maids if there were a dozen brownies to look after our castle."

"We pay the servants and maids, remember?" said Anne. "If the brownies were to do the job, the servants and maids would lose their jobs. Well, it seems there was a village on the other side of the waterfall, so he would go out from time to time and help out ... scatter seeds ... fan the farmers with his wings on a hot summer day and provide shade, things like that."

"I didn't know Tulp could be so awfully useful!" exclaimed Grace, sitting straighter with sparkling eyes. "He surely doesn't look the type to do those things."

"Yeah, but then the people started to leave ..."

"– Why did they leave?"

"Tulp didn't know," said Anne, frowning at Grace's interr-uptions. "After all, he's just a dragon."

"He should have explained his situation when we first met," Grace muttered darkly. "He was aggressive enough for us to panic, don't you think? *Fire*, and all that stuff ..."

"Tulp didn't know," continued Anne, "but I've read in the history book that people abandoned villages to move into castles and fortresses because of the growing threat of the Feirns. Sometimes families went on their own into the Forest, not knowing what would befall them, because they were afraid of moving into castles in case the castle might fall to the numerous Feirns. It is said that even one of the princes of Quindeli was seen as far as the mountains."

"Where's Quindeli?"

"Quindeli is to our castle's west, one of the Tenant Kingdoms, while the mountains are to the north-east," said Anne, and Grace wrinkled her nose again, due to the fact she didn't like geography and Anne had sounded like a geography textbook gifted with a mouth, which in her opinion was the unluckiest combination on earth. "And so. Feirns did come, and they took the remaining villagers away as prisoners. And Tulp grew lonely. It seemed no fun playing with the butterflies."

"How can anyone tell if Tulp played with butterflies, or what he felt about it?" said Grace with a scowl. "Insane, that is."

"I told you, he *told* me."

"*That's* the real question I don't get," snapped Grace. "How *can* he tell you?"

Anne looked at Grace, as if she was pondering how to explain an incredible story to a determined sceptic. Grace didn't like that expression and pointedly scowled.

"It's kind of like you see flashes of pictures in your mind," Anne said slowly, trying to explain as best as she could. "Like when you daydream. Like it's your memory, I mean, not like real flashes of pictures. So, specifically speaking, Tulp didn't *literally* tell me, but he did tell me."

Grace was thoughtfully silent for a while.

"So, you're saying he shared his memory with you?" said Grace at last.

"Yeah."

"But why did Tulp keep making orange fire and blast me away?"

"Did he?" asked Anne, frowning. "I suppose that could be the side effect caused by sharing his memories to me."

"Ha," grumbled Grace. "I was knocked unconscious each time you spent a nice time seeing his happy memories. How unfair. Wish he could have shown me."

"Maybe you looked aggressive?"

"Maybe *you* just looked excessively wimpy," said Grace sourly. "You don't have to voice all your truthful thoughts, Anne."

"Okay," said Anne apologetically. "So, he was circling over the village one day when he saw the golden eagle glint in the sky and decided to follow it."

"I think I read about the golden eagle somewhere ..."

"The golden eagle foretells great things about to happen and is said to lead the person who saw it to those happenings. Again, Tulp didn't know, but when at last he lost sight of the eagle, he was actually in Quindeli."

"I bet that useful bit of information was in another old, dusty, heavy history book."

"Indeed," said Anne indifferently. "When he flew down, the people panicked at the sight of him. Maybe they mistook him for Cairdew."

"Which I cannot understand at all, since Tulp and Cairdew

have entirely different coloured scales," snorted Grace. "Cairdew is red, while Tulp here is a ... a murky brown sort of colour. Not that it's unattractive, of course."

"Not at all," said Anne. "Cairdew's scales were the colour of murky brown, as you put it."

"Not so!" said Grace, getting excited. "Remember the wall painting by the library? You can't possibly forget it, actually, since we see it practically every day. So, you must know that Cairdew is painted red. Now, the artist, Gelert something or other, is a famous painter, and that is why some ancestor of ours would have asked him to paint that there. A mistake like this must have damaged his career!"

"Yes so," Anne replied grinning from ear to ear. "*Gelrit* something or other, if you see his other paintings, didn't always use practical colours. Painting Cairdew red was his way of expressing the ... the fire, and malicious energy ..." She paused. "I seem to have lost the ability to express in words skillfully, right now. Excuse me. I guess you understand though, despite my feeble explanation, right?"

"Yes," said Grace, "but in my opinion your explanation was by no means feeble."

"The people I was talking of cast iron nets at him, which I doubt did any good, but anyway the ruler of Quindeli sent a messenger to King Feridan, who summoned his daughter. She cast a spell, which bound Tulp to the earth, and Tulp was put in an underground dungeon."

"Wait – Isn't Quindeli supposed to be ruled by a king?" said Grace. "Why did the *ruler* call for King *Feridan*?"

"Before Tulp had arrived at Quindeli, the Feirns had already conquered the land, and King Therim, the son of Tenant Grethim, had been killed because he wouldn't submit to Feridan," said Anne. "Feridan had chosen a ruler for Quindeli. Rumors were that one day the descendant of Lilian would cut the ropes that bound Tulp and set him free, but of course, people didn't want that to happen. Later, Lilian's son Adren led his army to Feridan's kingdom. He also used the strong fortresses of Tertalin many times when waging battle. He recovered Quindeli and found a suitable heir for the empty throne, but –"

"Sorry, but can we perhaps skip to the main part?" asked Grace. "I know you like all this storytelling and everything, but I want to know right now how Tulp is supposed to be a good dragon."

"Oh," said Anne. "Okay. It was when the men of Tertalin were helping to clear the rubble at Quindeli and sorting out the stones they could use again for rebuilding when one of the King's advisors, who had been walking around the scene to see how things were, accidently discovered the entrance to the underground dungeon by falling into it. He met Tulp there and spent two weeks getting back out. There was no food in the underground tunnel, so the advisor made sure that food was brought to him as soon as he reached the castle to organize it. There had been chaos because of the sudden disappearance of the advisor, whose name was Didlit Didlum."

"Didlit Didlum?!" cried Grace. "I know him – so many fairytales are written by him! *He* was once an *advisor*?!"

"Yeah," said Anne. "When he retired, he wrote many fairytales."

"But why did the people of Quindeli panic, even if they had mistaken Tulp for Cairdew?" said Grace. "Their land was already under Feridan's control, plus Cairdew was supposed to be guarding the entrance to the prisons of Arcebrel at that time!"

Anne shrugged.

"Anyway, you must be aware that there are many versions of Tulp stories," she said.

"Yeah," Grace agreed. "That's why we panicked in the first place."

"I think those frightful legends began in Quindeli. I remember how surprised I was at how differently Didlit Didlum wrote of Tulp. I bet Tulp's shown him his memories too."

"What about the people of Quindeli then, if they believed Tulp was a fearsome dragon?" said Grace. "Either they would have stopped Didlum feeding the dragon, or they would have had enough sense to realize Didlum survived every time he went to feed Tulp, so Tulp can't be the monster they think of."

"Yes," said Anne. "So, Didlum managed to keep things secret with the king of Tertalin, who was, at that time, still Tenant Fridence."

"Ha ha," said Grace. She lazily fiddled her shoelaces into a huge knot. "I really wonder, did that work? Like, why would the king of Tertalin and his advisor stroll about every so often to Quindeli?"

"That's why they dug a tunnel."

"What – they dug a *tunnel* from here to there to feed a hungry dragon?"

"Yeah," said Anne. "But the good thing was, there was already a tunnel going halfway from here to Quindeli, due to a plan of making a passage in the times the Great Forest was dangerous, but it came to a stop. So, they only had to dig a bit further. And we've passed through the tunnels, haven't we?"

"Then you mean to say ..." said Grace, her face turning rigid, "we're in the underground dungeon? We're in Quindeli?!"

Anne grinned at Grace, who jumped to her feet and started hopping up and down, yelling, "We're in Quindeli! Hear it? Ya!"

"The existence of Tulp was totally forgotten as Advisor Didlum and King Fridence both passed away," said Anne. "Then our father came and discovered the tunnel. When he first saw Tulp, Tulp was in a deep sleep because he was on his way to death by starvation. Dad woke him up and began feeding him, and he grew to be friends with Tulp. Then he met a descendant of Feridan, owning Tieral's lamp. He grew troubled by it and made a decision that he would get back the lamp in any way, even with breaking the friendship with Tulp and stealing the queen's ring to swap it for the lamp, for that was the only thing that the woman descended from Feridan would swap for the lamp."

"The lamp of *Tieral*?" asked Grace. "Wait, how did Dad meet a descendant of Feridan?"

"Tulp didn't know that."

"How did Tulp know all the things Dad planned to do to gain the lamp?"

"Dad told him," said Anne. "I saw him in the shadows and listened to him talk about it to Tulp, because Tulp shared that memory with me too."

"So, why're we here, then?" said Grace, still on her feet, but not hopping around anymore. She was now examining the knotted shoelaces rather soberly.

"We have to help Tulp."

"Exactly," said Grace, endeavoring to untie the knots. "Exactly, how are we going to help Tulp? We're not some descendant of Lilian, are we? We *are* the descendants of one of Lilian's officers, of one of his *Tenants*."

"I admit that," admitted Anne, looking a little flustered. "But I was thinking of going to Finadel to bring a descendant of Lilian."

"The descendant of Lilian is most likely going to be the King himself," Grace pointed out. "Why did Tulp carry you here in the first place? Did Tulp tell you?"

"He let us know about what Dad did and what he's after, right?" said Anne. "If we free Tulp, he can be our evidence. We'll go back through the tunnel and travel to Finadel on the horses in the stables."

"Oh," said Grace, looking rather anxious.

"What's the matter?" said Anne, peering at her.

"Nothing," said Grace, adverting her eyes. Anne waited. "Oh, well, if you must know, the tunnel collapsed."

Anne looked stunned.

"Then ... how will we get out?" she murmured, looking extremely worried.

"There's that opening," suggested Grace, pointing to the hole high up in the ceiling.

"I don't think we can reach so high," said Anne. "Maybe we could search for the hidden entrance that Didlit Didlum fell into."

"Really?" said Grace, surprised. "I thought the entrance was that opening."

"If that opening was the entrance," said Anne, "I think he'd have fainted half way down and died the instant he reached the ground, since it's so high up."

Looking around them, they couldn't see how there could be an entrance in the cave walls.

"Maybe it got blocked up from the outside," said Grace, rubbing her chin. "Or maybe, we can't see it from the inside? Because if this is an underground dungeon, the people inside aren't supposed to be able to get out, right?"

"But then how did Didlit manage to get out?" said Anne. "He must have found the way out, because when he fell in, it was before there was any other way out, since it was later that he made the tunnels we passed through."

"How long did it take him to find the entrance that he came from?" asked Grace.

"Um, two weeks."

"How long do you think it'd take two people who haven't even come through that entrance to find the entrance?"

Anne was silent.

"Didn't Tulp see where Didlit Didlum fell into here?" asked Grace. "If we could see that, or when he finally found the entrance to leave, we could find it easily."

"Nah, he didn't see," said Anne. "Look ... If we freed him, he could get us up and out the opening."

"You told me only the descendant of Lilian can free him," said Grace.

"Yeah, but that's just rumors," said Anne dismissively. "It's worth a try, don't you think?"

"You mean to say there's nothing else for us to do than to try, even though we're not descendants of Lilian," said Grace with an exasperated smile. "Of course, I get what you mean."

Anne and Grace climbed the scales of Tulp and wandered around on top of the dragon, searching for the ropes that bound Tulp. Anne climbed down to the ankle parts. Suddenly she tripped and fell face first to the ground.

"Hey, what did you do that for?" said Grace, chuckling, walking down the leg. "It was hilarious!"

She had intended to jump down beside Anne, but something caught her leg and sent her sprawling, face down. She landed on top of Anne.

"You should really say that to yourself!" said Anne, pushing her off, trying to stifle her laughter but not doing well. "It must be the string. We couldn't see it, and that is why we tripped."

"Good thinking, but you found that out now?" said Grace.

Anne frowned at Grace.

"I found that out just now too," Grace ended, sending a satisfied grin back to Anne's cheeks. They both climbed cheerfully back up the leg and felt around for the string.

"Here!" said Anne and Grace together.

Grace was somehow holding Anne's hair.

"*Ow*," complained Anne.

"Oh, maybe not this ..." Grace said, letting it go disappointedly.

"Grace, here!" said Anne again, waving her fist before Grace.

"Hey, you're joking," said Grace. "See, there's no string, just your fist!"

"Silly, the rope is invisible!" replied Anne. "Hold it! Look, I mean, here, feel it. I've actually got it!"

"Don't call me silly," said Grace grumpily.

"Sorry," mumbled Anne. "Now, can you hold it for me?"

While Grace held the string, Anne felt for the knot. At last she found it.

"Here!" cried Anne, nearly sending Grace, who had been snoozing, tumbling backwards down the leg. The barely awake Grace crawled up beside Anne and felt the knot.

"Wow," said Grace, now wide awake with awe as she couldn't put her hand through what looked like nothing but air. "How strange it is to see nothing but to feel something."

Suddenly, she grasped Anne by the neck and shook her.

'She's excited with a new idea,' thought Anne.

"I've got a brilliant new idea!" said Grace, and she reached into her bag.

Out came a bottle of spray paint.

"How did no one think of this before?" Anne exclaimed with great excitement. "You are a genius! I absolutely cancel the 'silly' earlier on."

"I always was," said Grace, smiling poshly at Anne, who was busy frowning at Grace again. "I'm surprised you didn't discover it earlier, with your intelligence."

"I think I'm supposed to be flattered because what you said means I'm intelligent, but why does it seem so annoyingly sarcastic?" said Anne, with a slight bit of sarcasm in it.

"Because I was being sarcastic," Grace replied, examining the lid-less bottle of spray-paint and looking back inside her bag with an expression of horror. Anne nudged her, and Grace began spraying. Four seconds later, there was a visible rope in front of them. A few of Tulp's scales had been painted red in the process, but Grace decided that couldn't be helped. In nearly no time at all the knot was untied.

"Looks like rumors are rumors, eh?" said Grace, chuckling and nudging Anne with her elbow. "After all, it's not that hard to untie a *knot*."

They made their way down Tulp's leg. Tulp was still sleeping.

"Tulp?" said Anne loudly.

Grace sat down, leaning against Tulp's side. Anne waited, but Tulp didn't respond.

"Maybe he's still tired," said Anne. She looked around at Grace. "Grace?"

Grace was fast asleep. Anne shook her. She tried tickling. There was not even a grunt as a respond, which was strange, since usually Grace laughed in her sleep. Then Anne caught sight of some golden dust floating in the air.

"Epir's dust!" she exclaimed. "But how is it that I'm still awake?"

She slumped to the ground next to her sleeping sister and slapped lightly a few times upon her cheeks.

Anne leaned against Tulp wondering what she was supposed to do, wondering if this was it and she would have to wait desperately for the rest of her life with no rescue available. The ten days were as good as over, not a subject worth mentioning. This was a sleep like death; Grace and Tulp would sleep forever ... till the end of the world. She felt all the nervous tension that yesterday morning had brought begin to sink, along with her heart.

Then she looked up. It was as though someone had aroused her, by touching her on the shoulder. The cave grew suddenly brighter as golden light flooded in. It was as if the sun was setting into the cave. A few light pink petals drifted in through the open space in the ceiling, along with a cool, gentle breeze.

Anne got up to her feet and stretched out a hand to touch one of the soft petals. She didn't know why she did so; it was just irresistible. The petal stayed on the tip of her finger for a moment, then melted away. A whirl of light-coloured petals floated down and touched the ground. As the petals settled down, Anne could see a fair young woman with timeless beauty. It was as if she had solidified from the petals around her. Her dress was mossy green, and she wore a short brown, hooded cape. Her ash blonde hair was long and wavy, gently dancing along with the breeze. She had hazel eyes, and on her head was a crown of flowers. She was holding a brown drawstring bag in one hand, and a piece of folded paper in the other.

"I see your friends are in a deep sleep, Anne," she said with a smile, as if calling her name was something very pleasant. Her voice was sweet and soft. Anne was so astonished that she only stared at her for a moment.

"Yes," said Anne at last. Who was this fair woman? "Excuse me, but who ... who are you?"

"Oh," the woman said, taking a step forward. "I'm Tepiraniel."

— CHAPTER SIX —

To the East

Instantly, Anne dropped down and kneeled in front of Tepiraniel. Tepiraniel looked surprised. Then she hastily took Anne's hand and lifted her up.

"People shouldn't be praised by the title they are born with, but by the work they accomplish," she said. "It's by the deeds that they are judged."

"You did great things!" said Anne, in awe.

"I received much help," said Tepiraniel. "I received more help than I gave help. I come to you to give you help. A task is on your hands, and now you will do your part in saving others. I've written a poem to tell you and remind you what you must do to save yourself, your family, your friend here, and even your whole kingdom."

Tepiraniel handed Anne the piece of paper she had been clutching. It read:

These are times of trouble,
That may bring courage to rubble,
But if you master the fear,
You will save those dear.

With the wings you shall fly, with the cloak to hide,

Meet with her who for many years did bide.
Find the diamond from the witches' nook.
Go to the mountains, find the greedy duke.

With the snow of summer, from those eyes prying,
Rescue the king close to dying.
And bring the petal of water
From the land far east, to Lilian's daughter.

"How can I know what to do by this poem?" said Anne. "I'm sorry, but I can't understand."

"First, I'll be giving you some gifts," said Tepiraniel, opening her bag. "Then you might find it easier to understand." She pulled out what looked like four very large autumn leaves weaved together to form a shape of wings. "These are the wings of Belmer."

"You're giving this to me?" said Anne, carefully receiving the wings and examining it curiously. She felted awed at the thought that these were the very wings Belmer flew with so long ago.

"I'm merely passing them on to those who need it," said Tepiraniel. For a moment, she lowered her eyes and was silent. Anne looked concerned for her. Then Tepiraniel reached into her bag again. "Now, this is the cloak that conceals the wearer."

She handed a folded cloak to Anne. The cloak was the colour of juniper green. Anne had read that long ago Tepiraniel had recieved it as a gift, and she glanced at Tepiraniel, sorry that she should take away such a precious object. Tepiraniel smiled at her as if she knew what she was thinking.

"It's your possession now that I've given it to you," she said.

"Now, the first stop should be the Lake of Tears. Then you must find the ashes of water, for they will show you the way to go. It'll be plain, what you must do. And finally, I give you this necklace."

Tepiraniel gave Anne a silver necklace with a shell of a small clam.

"When you find the diamond, put it in this shell," she told her. "If you don't want the shell to open, it will not yield to any amount of force. The cloak only works when you put the hood on."

Tepiraniel gave a brooch to Anne, who put the cloak on, then pinned on the brooch.

The silver brooch was made of clear crystals twisted together with silver. It resembled a water petal, though Anne couldn't be sure since she had only seen drawings of the real thing.

"You must go now," said Tepiraniel. "I must go too. First fly north-east, and afterwards you will find the Lake of Tears."

"How shall I know which way is east?" asked Anne in an expression of bewilderment and worry. "I haven't brought my compass with me."

"Float your petal over water," answered Tepiraniel, handing a flat, transparent, circular container that held water to Anne who floated the brooch gently upon the water. She closed the lid. "The petal's point will always head north. Now, put on your wings."

Anne did as she was told. She watched curiously as Tepiraniel closed her eyes. She rested her hands on Anne's shoulders. She opened her eyes and grinned at Anne.

"Now, you are ready to go," she said. Anne wondered how she was supposed to fly with the wings. She felt for a string to pull in order to fly, thinking there must be some sort of mechanism, but instead her hand rested upon a soft, fluttering material. She looked behind to look at her back and was very surprised to see a pair of fluttering wings very different from what she had received. It was transparent, with a slight golden tinge to it.

"Wow," said Anne. She tried to move the wings. "How do I control these wings?"

"It's like when you want to move your finger," Tepiraniel explained to her. "You have to feel it's part of your body, that you can move according to your will without thinking."

Anne was able to control the wings. She fluttered them, and then she even hovered a few inches above the ground before landing, breathless.

"I'm ready to go," she said to Tepiraniel excitedly.

"Go, then," said Tepiraniel, grinning at her excitement. "Meet me here in a week's time with the snow of summer."

"A week ... What day is it today, Tepiraniel?"

"Today is the fourth of December."

"Oh, then, I will do so. Goodbye!" said Anne as Tepiraniel waved, and she flew out of the cave through the gap in the ceiling.

It was very bright and fresh outside, especially after being underground for ... for how long? Since Grace and Anne had followed the King down the staircase into the ground on the second of December, they had been underground for two whole days. That meant Grace had run for at least a day in pursuit of Tulp.

Snow had not fallen on Quindeli – or otherwise, the snow had melted on the girls' way through the tunnels. Seeing the sun's position, Anne reckoned it was late morning. Checking the petal compass, she flew north-east.

She flew across the Great Forest, checking the compass every now and then. It was satisfying how fast she could fly with the wings. Though she controlled the wings like it was part of her body, her wings didn't tire like her legs would if she were to run. She wondered if this was what sailing in the sea felt like, with nothing but green and brown treetops spread below her.

Anne wondered what would appear when the forest ended. The Great Forest was great like its name, and she was beginning to feel rather thirsty and hungry. The wings were still so fast that Anne thought she could reach Finadel by the end of the day if she wanted to.

After the thrill of flying had finally past, Anne began to feel extremely bored. There was still nothing except green trees, and she no longer paid attention to the view beneath her. The sun was now setting. The sky was a brilliant color of orange, but Anne was in no mood to praise its beauty. She sighed big and long. At that particular moment, her stomach chose to rumble, and realizing how tired she really was, she landed in the Great Forest just below her.

Anne yawned, wandering around for a place to sleep. Nothing really came into her view, and the sky was getting rapidly dark, so she spread her blanket and lay on a large flat rock as soon as she saw it. She thought it would be safer to be invisible, so she put her hood on and closed her eyes to sleep.

Anne woke up in the next morning. She lazily opened one eye to let the other rest for a bit longer. Then she opened the other. She gave herself a good stretch before sitting up. She could hear the pretty twittering of birds and could see many trees, a stream, and frail flowers peeping up here and there. Everything felt new after the refreshing nap. Making a simple sundial, she reckoned it was around seven o'clock. Anne went to a trickling stream and quenched her thirsty throat. She filled her stomach with a lots of rowan berries and sat down again. On staring at the forest, her eyes caught movement, so she stood up and wandered about. She spotted a beautiful fawn, staggering.

Anne drew closer and closer to the fawn and stretched out her hand to touch stroke it. But the fawn flinched when her hand touched its back. There was an arrow stuck in her side. Murmuring soothing words, Anne plucked out the arrow and washed the wound with clean water from her flask. The wound had depth, and it was heartbreaking to see the little fawn bleed.

Anne stumbled around the forest to gather the right herbs, then squeezed up them up to stench the blood flow. She was just applying a mixture of other herbs to the wound when she heard a very faint whistling noise. Anne whirled around and grabbed ... just in time to catch an arrow. Anne looked around for an explanation. Then, out of the bushes came a person wearing a weathered, green cloak.

Underneath he was wearing a green thing looking like a tunic, a brown leather belt with a sword tucked in to the side, and a dark green pouch. He had dark green straps on his wrists, as well as some muddy green leggings and dark green boots. He was basically dressed all in green, and he had an arrow notched on his bow, grasped tightly between two fingers. On his back was strapped a whole quiver filled with arrows. If he had an age, he looked the same age as Anne, but it was hard to tell because he somewhat *felt* to be much older than he looked. Anne couldn't see the colour of his hair, since he had his hood on.

Looking at the arrow that Anne was holding, that seemed to be hovering above ground of its own accord, he anxiously rubbed his eyes and blinked. He stepped cautiously out of his hiding place, ready to shoot at any time. He drew close to Anne, who had already dropped the arrow, looking this way and that.

"Who are you?" said Anne harshly.

The person let out a small "argh!", and nearly stumbled over. He pointed his arrow directly at Anne according to Anne's voice, breathing rather shallowly and looking this way and that. Anne walked up to him and knocked his bow out of his hands. She held the person by the collar, and though she couldn't lift him off his feet, she shook him as hard as she could.

"What are you doing?" she hissed. "First you shoot the poor fawn, and then you try to shoot me! Who *are* you anyway?"

"Who ... who is it?" he stammered, utterly amazed as well as utterly horrified to find his collar yanking at him. "I can't see you."

Anne flung him to the ground, and the person picked himself up and brushed his clothes. A moment later, he could see Anne, for she had thrown off the hood of the invisibility cloak that she had put on before falling asleep.

"I am Anne, from Tertalin. Who are you?" she asked in a defiant air. The person stared at Anne in disbelief.

"You ... have the cloak of Tepiraniel! How come –"

He was interrupted by Anne, who cleared her throat.

"I told you, I'm Anne. Introduce yourself!"

The person tried to regain what seemed to be his former posture and forced his chin up.

"I am Fluendel, son of –"

He dropped short when he was cut off.

"I'm not asking you whose son you are," Anne said in a wavery stiff voice meant to sound proud, looking down at Fluendel for a moment. She swallowed. Then she noticed Fluendel's long, blonde hair, for his hood had fallen off, and she faltered. She asked hesitantly, "Are you a girl?"

Fluendel's jaw dropped open involuntarily.

"No, what makes you think that?" he said, helplessly.

"Your ... your hair is long and blonde, and it's so neat that it seems you've combed it," stammered Anne. "Your face definitely doesn't suit a girl though, as well as your stature – Wait, you said ... you said you're a son."

"I'm not a girl," said Fluendel, closing his jaws. "Neither do I brush my hair. I'm an elf."

Brandishing his sword and running up a rock, flipping backwards and slashing with his sword, he landed gracefully on the ground and did a bow. He put his sword back into his scabbard.

"Your show was very impressive, but not at all needed except for bragging," said Anne with a bored tone, while she secretly sized up the elf with the corners of her eyes. Then she crouched down in front of the lying fawn to finish dressing the wound. "Anyway, you can't be an elf, can you? Elves are short and have funny, curved shoes, as well as a dangly-belled hat. But you're very different ... Wait, oh, maybe humans have been mistaking how the elves really look like!"

She couldn't hide her excitement, and rather awkwardly assumed her uninterested air, clearing her throat once or twice and looking away.

"Good, you found out something very obvious," said Fluendel, clapping his hands sarcastically and obviously feeling pleased that Anne had shown her embarrassment. It seemed to have been a shock for him, however, to be mistook for a girl, because he reached for his dagger and hacked off his long blonde hair rather roughly. Anne watched as locks of golden hair fell to the ground. Then she quietly put Fluendel's sword onto her belt. Fluendel spotted his sword, and his eyes grew wide.

"But ... but how?" spluttered the elf, losing all the jerkiness in his manner for the moment, "It was just in my scabbard and ..." He looked at his empty scabbard. Then eyeing the hand Anne had placed casually on the hilt of his sword, Fluendel put his hand defensively on his dagger while taking a step backward.

"I'll return yours if you give me another like it," said Anne with a smile, putting on Fluendel's scabbard since she didn't want to accidently cut herself after all.

"Hey!" said Fluendel, realizing that Anne had also taken his scabbard.

"Take me to your dwelling place, please," said Anne, taking up her bag and slinging it back on.

"Well, it's far away, and I'm not going to show you ..." said Fluendel, backing still further away. But to Fluendel's disappointment, Anne marched confidently off towards the north-east. Fluendel stood for a moment, staring at Anne. Then he rolled his eyes, shaking his head, and followed Anne.

They seemed to have come to the end of the Great Forest, for now Anne could see the open sky above a hill so large that it hid the sun. She ran up and up. It seemed that she was going the right way, since Fluendel didn't smirk but gloomily followed her. When she had reached the top of the large hill, she could see a few more hills spread out under her. A castle came into her view, its grey stones glowing gold in the sunlight. Fluendel caught up with her. Glancing at him, Anne could see he was really proud of the castle.

"Is that where you live?" Anne asked, and Fluendel nodded. "It looks magnificent."

"Thanks," said Fluendel, and they headed down.

When they had reached the hill bottom, they were overtaken by a group of elves in gleaming armor on armored stallions. The group of four, with one leading them, slowed down when they had reached Anne and Fluendel, which made Anne rather nervous.

"Prince Fluendel," called the leader. Anne widened her eyes. "Your father will not be happy about this."

"Well, he's busy, isn't he?" said Fluendel, going on his way without being bothered. "You don't have to weigh him down." He noticed Anne was peering at him. "Oh, Anne, this is Gilmor ... Commander Gilmor, this is Anne from Tertalin."

Anne and Commander Gilmor both nodded politely to each other. Anne thought he was very polite not to ask questions. Then Anne nudged Fluendel.

"What did you do?" she asked in a hushed voice.

"I went hunting on my own, that's all," muttered Fluendel.

"Oh."

"Would you like to ride a horse?" asked Gilmor, ready to step off his nickering chestnut stallion. The stallion had a white speckle on its left front leg.

"I'm fine walking," mumbled Fluendel, trudging on.

"What's his name?" asked Anne.

"Gilthor," said Gilmor, smiling at Anne as if pleased he was asked.

She looked around at the other three stallions. One was white with grey speckles, one was grey, and one was chestnut brown with a white speckle on his left front leg, just like Gilthor.

"Are they twins?" asked Anne.

"Yes," answered Gilmor, and Anne was reminded of herself and Grace.

"You could go, you know," said Fluendel, glancing at Gilmor. "I mean, you must be busy too."

"Priorities first," replied Gilmor. He and the other elves slid off their horses, emphasizing the point. The castle was much closer, looming above them, getting higher and higher as they drew near. Then they came to a stop.

"I've never seen such a place before," Anne stated.

In front of her was a stone wall with huge, crystal gates. The crystal gate was taller than the wall, and lines of crystal intertwined with each other in a beautiful pattern. Through the gates, she could see the castle. The walls of the castle looked a little weathered, with ivy and other vines climbing upon the surface. Anne stepped slowly up to the wall and placed her hands on the sparkling gate. Then she pushed.

"Wait ... Anne," said Gilmor, moving forward.

The big gate opened, and she stepped in, looking around at Gilmor questioningly. He seemed to hesitate, then he just led his horse Gilthor in after Fluendel.

Everything seemed to be in slow motion here in the elf world as it was so peaceful and quiet. Seeing elves practicing archery, and others practicing sword skills, however, it seemed rather odd that in such a peaceful paradise the elves seemed well prepared for, and perhaps expecting, war. The elves who had escorted them having armor even on their horses, which was rather disturbing. She wondered why, if it was so peaceful as it looked, the elves were training themselves to fight.

"Your father is talking with Nerisene," Gilmor said to Fluendel. He nodded once to Anne, and they parted ways.

There were many groves of trees, and the ground was covered with fallen leaves above the grass. Some trees were in full bloom while some trees shedding their brown leaves. It was a curious thing to see.

There were many trickling streams, where elves sat by the banks to drink. Anne noted that there was a very large pile of stones, near to a stone arch connected to the castle. She had no time to ask about that, because Fluendel whisked her away. She wanted to stay more and look, but Fluendel nudged her and led her into the castle through a small doorway in the wall. He led her through a dimly lit corridor and out into another corridor, but this one with one side open to some kind of courtyard. On second thoughts, it looked rather large and lush to be just a courtyard, but it was enclosed within the castle walls. Anne touched the arch columns as they passed by.

"Where is this place?" she asked. "I mean, this land – what do you call it?"

"We call it Admon Loriens," said Fluendel.

Out there was a place separated with arches and pillars, looking like the ruins of a tiny Colosseum, where a little fountain bubbled in the center of it and cracked marble benches lining in between the arches. There, two elves were in conversation.

"... a mortal cannot find their way inside," said one of the two, a male elf dressed in brown robes embroidered with silver. A simple crown of silver rested on his forehead. "Well, a little girl did, but ... I don't know, we all don't know how she managed to pass through. Surely the prophecy didn't mean the little girl, for nothing has changed after she came and went."

"Do you mean to say the Feirns cannot enter, my King?" asked the other one, an older, frail female elf leaning on a crooked staff that looked rather gnawed and heavy. She gathered her robes around her and watched the male elf pace about on the grass. "The Feirns are, after all, mortals, aren't they?"

"Yes, but no," said the male elf, pausing to look at the elderly person. "The Feirns will be able to pass through the gate, because they are different; they aren't just mortal in the ordinary term. Their souls are tied to the stone, and that gives them a different quality."

The female elf nodded. "Same here. She has different qualities."

The male elf was silent for a while.

"Do you know anything concerning my daughter?" he said at last.

"What about her?"

"Is she alive?" he said. "Where might she be?"

"We cannot be sure," said the female elf, thoughtfully.

"Why hasn't she returned yet?"

"We cannot be sure about that either, but to guess, maybe she is still captive to her captivators, or else maybe she has lost her way ..."

"She won't be safe, even in the attempt to return," said the male elf, starting his pacing again. "We have no peace."

"So, it is that the girl will come, with the cloak of Tepiraniel, to bring peace to this weary land," said the old female elf, "You know this, my King; it is the prophesy of old, though no one had a single idea about what this meant before the times changed."

Just then, Fluendel walked over and nudged the elf in the grey cloak. The two elves turned to look at Fluendel and Anne in surprise.

"The girl has come!" muttered the female elf.

"Where's your hair gone?" said the male elf. He seemed ready to faint.

"Father, meet Anne," said Fluendel. Then he leant over and whispered, "She has the cloak of Tepiraniel."

The Queen gazed through the window at the already darkening sky, with an expression clearly expressing worry.

"It's nearly the end of their fourth day," she thought. "I wish I knew at least where they are."

She scanned the castle walls, glancing at the village and her eyes lingering longer at the forest. At length, seeing nothing moving, she looked away and stood up to face the rest of her queenly duties. The King had not yet returned.

When the Queen had turned her back on the window, the forest began to quiver and shake.

— CHAPTER SEVEN —

From the West

By the next morning, the castle of Tertalin was surrounded by a vast army. A great commotion broke out inside the castle walls as trumpets were sounded from all around them. A messenger was sent to the enemy camp, bearing a message from the Queen.

"Her Majesty the Queen of Tertalin asks by what reason you have come to war," said the messenger.

"Did the Queen say so?" said the veiled woman in an amused tone of voice. "Tell the woman in my castle, on *my* throne, that she is no longer Queen, and that the real Queen is here, right here waiting."

"How could you claim the Queen's throne?" the messenger said. "It is discourtesy to say so even before the war has begun! A person of no relation with this kingdom suddenly claiming the rights while our queen still breathes? That is insulting this whole kingdom."

"No relation?" whispered the woman. Then she smiled maliciously. "It is true that I have no blood relative – and I, for one, would be totally *disgraced* to have such a relative. But I agree that no other woman should claim the throne while the Queen still breathes!"

She held up her hand, showing clearly a ring upon her finger, a ring that had a little white diamond. The messenger's eyes grew wide for a moment, and the woman laughed contemptuously.

"So, you are the Queen's messenger?" she asked.

"I am."

"Then tell her to come down from my throne," she said, "for you are now my messenger."

"Even though you may have stolen that ring," said the messenger firmly, "a ring is merely a ring, and the hearts of our people stand firm to our rightful King and Queen – till the moment they let out their last breath!"

"Well said," the woman said coldly. "But your king is no more. To the last breath, you say? It is already over. According to your law, I am not an intruder. If Tertalin should uphold their own law, I am their rightful queen. If the people should not submit to their queen, their queen shall gladly make them submit. As for the war, I am not the one starting it – it has already been started a very long time ago."

Anne woke up at the sound of a bell gonging. When she opened her eyes, she was rather confused to see that she was on a silk bed. She had thought for a moment that she was back in Tertalin in her cozy bunk bed, listening to the tower clock. If she had counted correctly, and if she had started counting from the moment the bell starting gonging, the bell had sounded seven times.

'So, it's seven o'clock,' she thought.

Seven o'clock. Usually the rooster alarm clock would have woken her and her sister up, and then Grace would have made her brush her hair before she tied it up. Then they would have headed downstairs for breakfast to another common, pleasant day.

Sunlight was beaming through the silk curtains on the window upon her right. She walked to the curtain and drew it back, feeling the cool, morning breeze with closed eyes. Then she remembered last night, and she frowned thoughtfully. Beiron had seemed to be agitated by a reason Anne did not know. Even Fluendel seemed not to know, come to think of it.

Fluendel had shown her around the castle. They had returned to have a cup of tea with the old female elf, who turned out to be Nerisene. Nerisene was someone she would like to have near her, Anne thought. She made her feel comfortable, like with Granny, but in a different way. They ate dinner as a picnic on the meadows. Then Fluendel had shown her to this room where she was to sleep, and she had slept peacefully after a good dinner and hard thought. Presently, she changed into her jeans and T-shirt then went out of the room.

Anne wondered when the people here ... the elves ... ate breakfast. She hadn't brushed her hair or tied it, which made her feel rather guilty, but she was feeling rather cozy with her bushy hair surrounding her and blocking the light from her shut eyes.

Once out of the room, however, Anne brushed the hair out of her eyes with her fingers and went down the corridor, and down the stairs. She walked out into the open and enjoyed the pleasant feeling of the breeze filling her lungs while she stood in the warm sunlight. Some elves were already out, training with swords and bows again, reading books, or just talking.

Anne headed for a stream to wash her face, savoring its coolness. It seemed that the cool waters had restored her sleep-blurred eyes, and she looked around seeing everything clearly. Feeling fresh, she tied her hair by herself. Then she remembered Fluendel, wondering what he might be doing now, and she got up from the stone she had been squatting on by the stream.

Anne was thinking of going back to investigate his room, when she spotted two figures, one red-haired and one blonde-haired, making a soundless racket not very far away. Curiosity getting the better of her, she moved closer. Fluendel was sitting on a stool with someone standing over him, making snipping noises. Fluendel's hair looked white in the sunlight, and it was falling off him. As she drew closer, she could clearly hear the racket Fluendel was making.

Snip!

"Ow!" he hissed. "Feralene, you've snipped at my ear –!"

"Hang on, quit squirming, if you really want your ear whole!"

Snip snip!

"Seriously, keep it whole, I need my ears – DO NOT make me bald for a joke, it's not funny!"

"Keep still –"

The snipping person jerked Fluendel's head forward and held it firmly still as a demonstration.

Snip!

"Another lock! Seriously, are you planning to leave any hair on at all when you're finished? I *am* a prince!"

Fluendel finally caught sight of Anne and let out a yelp before grabbing the cloth lain around his shoulders to cover his face. Anne grinned, before looking to see who was cutting his hair.

"Oh, hi Anne! My, how you've grown!"

Feralene was a girl looking the same age as Anne with long hair that glowed like red-hot metal. As Anne wondered how she knew her name and whether they'd somehow met before, the girl seemed to catch herself, and she held out her hand.

"My name is Feralene, and I'm Fluendel's friend. Did you see him hack his hair off with his sword?" – (snip!) – "I thought –" (snip!) "– that he looked rather pitiful –" (snip!) "– with the ragged hair that was neither quite short nor long ..."

Fluendel gave a long groan, clutching his cloth to his face and sliding down the stool.

"There now, cheer up, you're done."

The first thing Fluendel did was gape at the amount of hair scattered on the floor, and then to clutch at the back of his head for hair. Then he grabbed a mirror and looked at himself with horror. He glanced back at Anne and thrust his head back into his cloth with a groan.

"Why?" said Anne, keeping a straight face and brushing off the hair from Fluendel's clothes. "I think it rather suits you."

"I thought she was cutting off all my hair!" said Fluendel, his hand returning to the back of his head. He seemed to be sobbing, yet not sobbing at the same time. Apparently, it seemed that he had never cut his hair short before, or he would not have made such a fuss about it. Then the bell that Anne had heard back in her room sounded again. For a moment, they stood still listening to it.

"Oh dear, we have to be on time for breakfast," Fluendel said suddenly, picking up the stool and running off. "Feralene knows where – you just have to follow her ..."

Anne and Feralene exchanged glances.

Breakfast was eaten in a vast hall, where a lot of important-looking elves ate. At the head of the table were two seats. King Beiron seated on the right seat, but the left seat remained empty. There was another empty seat, next to Fluendel, where Anne sat.

After a breakfast, Anne went out and enjoyed the sunlight, sitting on a rock, and was planning her journey when Fluendel came and joined her on the rock, still grabbing at his back hair.

"You aren't wearing your all-green suit today, I noticed," said Anne. Fluendel looked down at what he wore as if someone else had put them on him without his knowing. He had what seemed like a T-shirt looking one size too big for him made of something like sackcloth, a belt around the waist, and the usual sword was slung on that had been retrieved from Anne. He had black leggings with brown shorts, as well as brown boots on the feet. Fluendel shrugged absent-mindedly.

"So ... you're going?" he inquired.

Anne nodded.

"How did you know the way here, anyway?" he asked.

"I guessed," said Anne slowly, studying Fluendel's queer expression. "I was supposed to go north-east, so I guessed."

They were silent for a while, in which Fluendel studied a groove in his rock.

"Why are you going?" he said at last, peering up. "I mean, don't you like it here?"

"I like it here," agreed Anne. "But I have to go on my way."

"What is your mission anyway?" Fluendel shook his front hair out of eyes though it only came down to his eyebrows and couldn't reach his eyes. He looked as if he was regretting that he had cut off his hair.

Anne got out the piece of paper where the poem was written. Fluendel read it out loud, ending questioningly.

"My family is in danger right now," said Anne. "As well as my kingdom. My sister is especially dear and exceptionally close to me, and a friend of mine is also in danger."

Fluendel cocked his head sideways, puzzled.

"Why do you care about your family?" he said bitterly. "I don't, anyway. My dad doesn't care for me. He's always too busy to notice, especially now."

"What do you mean?" Anne said, surprised. "Families naturally have a love for each other ... that's what families are for, isn't it? Your dad may seem not to care for you, but I think he does, a great deal too, though his way of expressing it may be different from what you expect. Anyway, I understand that you feel neglected – why, my dad's a king, too! But I can't expect him to give me all his time when I'm not giving mine."

Fluendel chose the timing to hand her a sword just like his, inside a scabbard also looking the same, perhaps because he was feeling awkward about the subject. Anne adjusted the sword onto her waist with a very pleased expression. She unsheathed the sword and held it up, savoring the glint of sunlight upon the blade.

"So, this is an elven blade?" she said excitedly.

"Yeah," said Fluendel, "if you call it so."

"Thank you," she said sincerely, and Fluendel gave her a half-hearted grin. As she rose and ran to go and pack her stuff, Fluendel hurriedly called after her his words jumbling in his haste.

"At the gate!... Your belongings!"

Anne returned.

"Did you know, Anne?" said Fluendel truthfully. "Though you are kind of irritating, I found out that you're quite a good friend."

Anne pretended to be offended.

"Hey, I'm just being candid with you, I didn't mean to ..." he started, thoroughly tricked.

Too curious what Fluendel's sorry expression would be, Anne looked up and sniggered.

"If I had a brother, I'm sure he would be like you," she said, grinning broadly, which kind of annoyed Fluendel. "By the way, I don't know the way to the gate, so I'd be thankful if you lead me."

Fluendel went with her to the gate. He said goodbye by the gate and stood there, watching until Anne was out of sight, before climbing on to the wall to watch her further progress from above.

Anne dragged her heavy feet that were reluctant to leave the castle. She sighed. Of course, she wanted to stay there. But she had to save her dear sister, Grace. And everyone else, herself included.

"Grace is lucky to have a very faithful, kind sister who refuses much pleasure and goes on a hard quest to save her while she is sleeping peacefully in a warm cave," she mumbled to herself, and she laughed, remembering how Grace had run all the way to Quindeli from Tertalin, in the darkness of an underground tunnel, with the determination that she would defeat what she believed to be a dangerous dragon to save her. Even though Grace thought she might have already been gulped down, which then would make her pursuit useless – only a way to get gobbled up along with her sister, together to the death.

She looked back and saw that the whole castle was now disappearing over the hills, and as she went further down, she couldn't see the walls anymore. Anne sighed once more and kept walking. She plodded on and on until she sat down on a rock to rest and looked back once more. Now the hills could not be seen by the many trees shrouding it. She could hear a strange noise, like many trumpet horns being blown from far off. There was a distant rumbling sound, like many people were marching. As Anne stood listening for quite a while, she thought that the noise sounded a bit bigger.

"The Feirns!" said Anne aloud. She began to run back towards the castle. Then she stopped abruptly. The Feirns?! What was she thinking of? She must have read too many fairytales. It couldn't possibly be the Feirns. There had been no sound of them for many hundreds of years, as far as she knew. There had not been even rumors.

But then, who would be sounding these trumpets, and marching towards Admon Loriens, other than an army – and what army other than the Feirns?

The sounding of marching had become louder. Anne was overwhelmed with sudden panic that she started to run anyway, towards the castle, whether what she heard be the Feirns, or a great herd of lost antelopes, in which case would make her rather embarrassed.

Running like her life depended on it, which was probably close to the truth if it really were the Feirns coming behind her, she bounded up the hill. She was exhausted when she reached the top, but she easily raced downhill. Looking ahead of her, she could see the gates open, and a couple of people came out, both riding a horse. The people apparently seemed to have spotted her, because they galloped towards her.

The two people turned out to be Gilmor and Fluendel. Gilmor was riding Gilthor, while Fluendel was riding a horse she had never seen before. It was a white horse, with a wavy white mane. He was also wearing a dark brown cloak.

"Anne!" Fluendel yelled, looking rather worried as he saw her panting and running towards them. "You okay?"

"No!" she yelled back, stopping at last and taking deep breaths. Gilmor and Fluendel came to a stop in front of her. "Listen, I heard these strange noises ... trumpet sounds, and the sound of marching ... Do you perhaps think the Feirns are still around?"

Gilmor and Fluendel exchanged a glance. Then Fluendel nodded briefly, and Gilmor galloped away without even saying goodbye.

"He's gone to tell my father, so don't worry," Fluendel told Anne, getting off his horse. There was a silence, then Anne said, "Aren't you going?"

"You're kidding, right?" said Fluendel grinning. "You don't think I'd let you go on your own, do you, not when the Feirns are out there?" Seeing Anne's expression, he realized she had thought so. "I saw your progress was slow, so I thought I'd give you a ride."

He awkwardly looked at the ground, a hand on the back of his neck.

"Really?" said Anne, embarrassed. "Oh, then ... I'd very much like your company. Thanks."

"You don't mind riding at the back, do you?" asked Fluendel, getting onto his horse again.

"Of course, I don't," said Anne, taking his hand and clambering onto the horse's back behind Fluendel. "And I really do thank you."

— CHAPTER EIGHT —

The Lake of Tears

It was getting rapidly dark.

Then Anne leaned heavily against Fluendel's back. Silence passed. Fluendel didn't remember Anne being so silent, so he looked over his shoulder. Her eyes were closed as she leaned on his back, breathing softly and rhythmically. Anne was sleeping.

"When did you fall asleep?" he asked. Then he remembered that Anne would not be able to answer if she was sleeping.

Then he too fell asleep, and he would have fallen off the horse if Anne hadn't grabbed him.

"Who said to fall asleep, sleepy?" said Anne, chuckling and yawning at the same time. "You owe me one."

"Depressing, since you fell asleep too," said Fluendel grumpily.

"I was thinking," said Anne. "I don't really favor sleeping."

"You're welcome," said Anne a little while later.

"What?" said Fluendel.

"I just saved your life, right?" said Anne.

"Oh, yeah, thank you."

"You're welcome."

They rode for a while longer and night fell deeper. It was a wonder how the horse didn't tire as it galloped, and how it dared to gallop when it was this dark. Wondering if the horse could possibly have super night-vision, Anne patted the horse with gratitude.

"Don't you think we should rest, now?" she said. "The horse should be exhausted by now, and I'm really tired."

Fluendel agreed, and after they had found a nice, sheltered spot with a low tree to sleep under and the sound of water rushing somewhere nearby, they both slipped off the horse and left it to munch happily on the grass.

"I'm hungry," said Anne and Fluendel at the same time.

"Do you have food?" asked Anne. "Because if I had been more thoughtful, I'd have packed some. Which means I wasn't so thoughtful and have packed none."

"Sure, I have," Fluendel replied, removing a sack from the back of the horse, near the saddle, that Anne hadn't the leisure to notice before.

Together they ate a scanty meal and prepared to sleep. They collected wood and started a fire going.

"End of the second day," Anne mumbled to herself.

"What?" asked Fluendel.

"Huh?" said Anne. "Oh, I haven't told you fully! I have ten days in total to prove I haven't stolen the queen's ring, but that doesn't matter right now. Tepiraniel gave me a week to carry out the poem you've read, and today was the second day –"

"What's the queen's ring?" asked Fluendel.

"In the kingdom of Tertalin, the woman who has the queen's ring becomes Queen," said Anne. "Five days ago, the ring disappeared."

"Why does that matter?"

"It matters because I'm no ordinary person." Anne paused to make it more dramatic, as she was prone to do.

"Well, yeah, that's exactly what I've been saying – you are so strange ..." Fluendel said without noticing.

"That is not what I meant," said Anne with a tinge of disappointment in her voice at Fluendel's poor reaction. "I'm the princess of Tertalin."

Fluendel was lost for words, his mouth failing to form a speech.

"YOU are a ... a PRINCESS?" gasped Fluendel.

"Ha," said Anne, "Do I look like a savage?"

"Nope," said Fluendel soberly.

Anne smiled.

"So, I have to save my parents," she continued, "Since my parents are the King and Queen. The woman who has the ring becomes Queen when a new king sits on the throne."

"You mean the woman who has the ring can become Queen even though she's not married to the King?" asked Fluendel, shocked.

"Kind of ..." said Anne. "Like, the original plan of this law –"

"It's a law?!" said Fluendel, more shocked.

"Yes," said Anne. "The original plan of this law is to ensure that the Queen's position is not ignored. When all goes right, the King and Queen's son becomes the new king, and the former queen who is his mother gives the ring to his wife, the new Queen. But as you can guess, someone stole the ring – and my sister and I are certain our dad stole it, but he doesn't want it for himself. Sadly, it turns out that he's thicker than I ever thought. I don't know what's gotten into him ... why would he want to voluntarily place his life in such a dangerous position?"

"But why do you have to prove you haven't stolen it?" asked Fluendel. "You're their daughter. Isn't the ring going to be your possession anyway?"

"My sister was born before me," said Anne. "Dad used that to insist I must have stolen it, because if I wait, the ring would be passed on to the firstborn."

"Your dad did that?" said Fluendel. "And you're sure he's a very good dad who cares much about you? And you're worried for his safety? He chose this; you didn't. He must have considered the outcome."

"I don't know," said Anne, shaking her head. "My dad isn't the person to accuse me of anything. I don't think he knows what he's doing."

"I'll take first watch," said Fluendel.

"If you don't mind, I'd rather," said Anne. "I'm rather slow at falling asleep, so I need to tire myself out first with a little thinking."

"Sure," said Fluendel, with an uncertain smile, "but aren't you already tired? I think I heard you say so with your own mouth."

"Nah," said Anne, taking her place by the fire. "Sleep first."

Fluendel lied down to sleep. He watched Anne, who was poking at the fire with a stick. Something caught his eye. There was something fluttering behind Anne's back. It seemed to be a pair of delicate wings, faintly glittering gold. Fluendel was about to open his mouth to ask what those wings were, but in an instant, he had fallen asleep, and his thoughts grew murky.

The next morning, Fluendel woke up and opened his eyes with a start. Sunlight was streaming down on him. He closed his eyes to enjoy some more, but the instant he did so, the sunlight withdrew. Then he heard Anne's voice.

"Woke up now?" There was a soft nudge in his ribs. "Come and eat your breakfast!"

"Uh!" Fluendel mumbled sleepily. "I know who's making the shadows." Fluendel opened his eyes again and looked. Sure enough, there was Anne staring down at him, blocking the sunlight from him.

"I have only one request; move out of the sun!" said Fluendel.

"I am not Alexander, and you're SO not Diogenes, so ha," said Anne, grinning cheekily, blocking more light from the frowning Fluendel. "I have made breakfast."

"I heard," groaned Fluendel, heaving himself up into a sitting position. Anne nearly fell over.

"What?!" he exclaimed, eyeing her warily as she seemed to shake all over.

"Your ... your hair!" she managed to say, before laughing away.

"What's wrong with it?" mumbled Fluendel, rubbing his eyes

"I'll be waiting," said Anne weakly.

She walked across to where two small rocks were drawn beside a large, flat rock that seemed to be serving as a table.

Fluendel's stomach growled and threatened that he had better go and eat, or else ...

"Or else what?" grumbled Fluendel, but still he hurried to follow Anne for food.

"How come you didn't wake me?" said Fluendel, taking a seat. "Aren't you tired?"

"Well, as a matter of fact," said Anne, "I am not tired, because after an hour or two I reckoned that we didn't need to take turns watching for nothing."

Anne gave Fluendel a large leaf on which she had dumped something mashed together unceremoniously in a weird-looking lump, along with a forked twig. The leaf still had tiny droplets of water clinging to the surface, indicating Anne had washed it clean in the stream.

"What's this thing?" asked Fluendel, eyeing the mashed food suspiciously and prodding it with his forked twig.

"Try and guess," said Anne, looking pleased with her cooking. "You'll love it."

Anne scooped up a mouthful and shoved it in her mouth. She seemed to adore the taste. Fluendel followed her example in exactly the same way, as if he was worried that it would turn to poison if he ate it in another method or expression. He had a shocked look as he swallowed it and choked.

"Where did you get mashed potatoes?" he said, eagerly scooping up another mouthful. "It's so tasty! Although I do feel it needs milk since it's so dry."

"It's actually breadfruit," said Anne, licking her twig and leaf delicately clean. "Not potatoes."

"Oh," said Fluendel, looking flustered as he hurriedly finished his off.

They went for a drink in the stream. As Fluendel bent down, he could see his watery reflection upon the surface of the stream.

"Gosh," he stated. "This ... is why you burst out laughing?"

He observed the hair stuck up like a cockerel's comb with no words.

"I'll straighten it out for you," said Anne, and she went over to dunk Fluendel's head in the water, but unfortunately Fluendel had been gripping her wrist when he fell in. In the end, Anne got equally soaked.

"Sorry," gasped Fluendel.

They returned to the horse both dripping wet and gasping.

"Oh my," said Anne sadly as she sat down on the saddle with a squelch. "The horse couldn't feel very pleasant."

"I have a question," said Fluendel, reaching behind his back to squeeze his hair but then realizing his hair was short. He shook out the water in his hair like a dog instead and started the horse. "How come you have Belmer's wings?"

"How come you know? I forgot about it," said Anne, pausing in the midst of squeezing her hair, looking over her shoulder to see if the wings were on her back.

"I saw them when you were prodding the fire, just before I fell asleep," he explained.

"Oh, yeah, Tepiraniel gave them to me," said Anne. Fluendel looked envious. "But where have they gone now?"

"According to my theory, they're still there on your back, but they will not show when they are not needed," said Fluendel, looking flustered as if he had only just made up his theory.

The warm sunlight slowly dried out their wet clothes, though

Anne's hair stayed wet.

Now they came to a spacious forest. The forest was cool and refreshing. It had a stream trickling between the rocks, and there were a few flowers peeping up from under the fallen leaves. A little stream sparkled and seemed to glow in the colour of turquoise, moss covered the rocks and tree roots, and the dew on the leaves and petals glinted like jewels. When they had passed through the forest, at last they could see a lake.

The Lake of Tears. Anne had seen lakes only a few times in her life. She was used to small ponds, where she and Grace fed the ducks with bits of bread. Anne was transfixed with the sight of this lake, that was not familiar to her, but all the more awe-inspiring because of it.

The lake was crystal clear. An old willow tree stood bending over it as if to look at its own reflection.

While Fluendel was lost in the beauty of the lake, Anne silently slid down from the back of the horse and ventured to actually go there rather than just looking at it. Fluendel slipped off his horse, leaving it there to graze in the grass, and joined Anne. Both stood at the edge of the lake, which was so calm that the surface seemed to be made of glass.

"Your reflection looks way prettier than you," Fluendel said, peering at the surface of the water.

"Thanks," said Anne thoughtfully, "if that's a compliment."

She then looked around and instantly found what she was looking for. There was a waterfall on the other side of the lake from where they were standing.

"We should go there," said Anne, nudging Fluendel.

Fluendel looked up at the waterfall Anne was pointing at and caught his breath. It certainly looked as if there would be something on the other side.

"How are we supposed to get there?" said he, staring with his mouth hanging slightly open.

"Simple," said Anne, "We just have to swim –"

"In all these clothes!" said Fluendel. "No way, we would probably drown before we're even half way."

"I can swim like that, you know, but if you can't ..." Anne looked around as if to spot a better idea.

Fluendel opened his mouth. "We should make a boat and oars and –"

"It would take ages to make one, let alone cut one of these massive trees!" said Anne. "That would be worse than swimming with a fur coat on!"

A dull silence followed in which Fluendel agreed with Anne and each tried to think of another way. At last, Anne spotted something.

"Look there!" she said happily. "We don't have to make one." She pointed to a small boat that was floating on one side of the lake. "One's already made."

Anne and Fluendel ran to the boat. Anne got in. Fluendel tried to get in, but he fell in the water.

"Ugh!" he said, hastily getting out of the cold water and into the boat. "Even water seems to love me."

They began to glide through the water. At last, they came near the waterfall.

"What do we do now?" asked Fluendel, anxiously eyeing the

waterfall as they were drawn nearer and nearer.

"Brace yourself!" said Anne, her voice rising to a cry as they passed through the waterfall.

"Aw, man," complained Fluendel. "My clothes are wet again!"

Anne simply squeezed the water without a word from her dripping hair that she had just managed to dry. They were surprised by a jolt. The boat had bumped on a rock. Together they climbed out of the boat and set foot on shore in a shallow cave that had been concealed by the waterfall.

"What kind of place is this?" said Anne.

Fluendel shrugged.

"Find out for yourself," he said.

Anne went right up to the end of the cave ... and realized it wasn't really the end of the cave at all. There, though she didn't remember seeing it only seconds before, was a very wide tunnel gaping at her.

Anne slowly took a big step backwards. One moment, she could see the tunnel very clearly. The next instant, it was gone, and she was left facing the cave wall. She looked hard as the image flickered before her eyes, then turned around. Fluendel was looking at her with a rather puzzled expression. He grinned when he saw her flushed cheeks, though he didn't know what had caused such an excitement.

"Come over here!" she exclaimed, so impatient that she went over to pull him to the spot. "Please," she added.

Fluendel's mouth dropped open, and he exclaimed, "Oh!"

But looking at the threateningly dark tunnel, Fluendel began to back down, nearly falling in the water again. Anne bracingly grasped Fluendel's arm and dragged him in with her into the tunnel despite his protests.

Inside, it was kind of very dark. They kept going.

"What is the matter with this –" said a frustrated Fluendel, but Anne didn't hear the rest of his sentence as both were suddenly drenched by a waterfall. They slipped and fell into another lake, and suddenly all was so bright. Anne and Fluendel swam out of the lake with great difficulty and lay in a panting heap on the grass.

"What were you saying?" gasped Anne.

Then her eyelids closed, and she fell asleep.

After the short but very reviving sleep on the grass in the warm sun, Anne and Fluendel woke up to see that their clothes had dried. They stood up and looked around them at last.

This side of the tunnel was fairly different from the other side. The side where Anne and Fluendel had come from had been silent in a sorrowful way, but this side seemed peaceful, more like the energy flowing out from new life. More flowers. Brighter. The lake of this side was also smaller, somewhat friendly.

Anne could hear birds twittering somewhere up in the trees. Butterflies fluttered gracefully among the flowers. Being strengthened by the nap, Anne and Fluendel stepped into the forest. The forest was very refreshing. It was a strange thought, but it really seemed as if the forest understood feelings. Anne sat down suddenly with a confused look on her face. Fluendel was so surprised that he yelled out.

"Whatever's the matter with you?" said Fluendel after he had dropped down beside Anne with a concerned look mixed with shock on his face.

"I had this feeling before," she said, the corner of her lips curling up into a smile. "It's inexpressible, but I know this feeling – I feel it when I'm I such a place as this or something. I have a picture that I do not know what the whole looks like, yet I know it and I know it's there. I get this tingling feeling that makes me sad and I wish to hold to that moment forever, but of course, like always, it is so brief that it is even hard to recall. I think it's an image of what I lost, in the past. And now everywhere around me, I am feeling that tingling; the tingling this time doesn't stop – and I can remember this part of my hidden memory. I am in that place, and it makes me so glad!"

"I'm glad that the thing that made you collapse was gladness," Fluendel said slowly, "but I can't understand your complicated talk. The tingling feeling makes you sad, but you want it? Or is that you want it, but it doesn't come because it is hidden, but you know it, but you don't ..." He looked a little confused.

"I'm confused," said Anne.

"Me too," Fluendel agreed. "But I've understood that the thing overwhelming you is gladness! I wonder what the hidden memory of the delightful past is."

Then suddenly Anne gasped. Fluendel gave a start.

"What is it?" Fluendel exclaimed.

"It's nothing, I'm sorry," gasped Anne, looking at Fluendel, then laughing at his expression, "I just realized that this must be the place Tulp had been before he was captured."

Fluendel sat down on a big tree root, exhausted.

"Really, you shouldn't keep on frightening me like that, Anne! I thought something serious had happened! You mustn't do that again, or I might not believe you when it is *really* urgent. Promise me not to do that again."

Fluendel made Anne promise, who stopped grinning when she saw his seriousness. Fluendel found his energy again very soon, and he jumped up to his feet to keep going.

"What are we supposed to do here? I forgot the poem thingy," said Fluendel, looking expectantly at Anne, who rummaged for the paper holding the precious lines. It was all melted into one piece.

"Oh my gosh!" Anne squealed, at which Fluendel was shocked again, then looked very frustrated at himself having lost concentration because of a delicate brown flower he hadn't seen before.

"I'm really sorry," Anne said hastily, patting Fluendel on the shoulder who had sat down on a log, "I didn't know you had such a flibbity heart."

"I'm *sure* there's no such word," said Fluendel with exasperation, "But WHAT was it this time?"

"The poem's all ruined – well I'm not sure, but it's all in one lump," said Anne, peering down at Fluendel's horrified face. "It must have melted down in my pocket when we were drenched in that waterfall, and it must have hardened when we dried out in the sun!"

"Then do you have any idea what we are supposed to do next?" he spluttered, clasping his head in his hands.

"Luckily, if I think hard, I think I will be able to remember," said

Anne, she too sitting down next to Fluendel.

"Well, that is a lot of uncertain thoughts," said Fluendel glumly.

Anne tried to recall the next line, while Fluendel looked at Anne expectantly.

"So?" he asked at length.

"Huh?" said Anne. "Uh, no."

"You mean you haven't managed to remember?"

"Yeah ..."

"Now what should we do? You have to go on your quest if you're going to save everyone, but we don't know what we have to do for our quest!"

"Isn't there a way to un-lump this thing? I mean, that's our only chance, right?"

"Yeah, but that's basically ... the same as no chance ..." said Fluendel, suddenly looking rather sympathetic. "That lump of paper has gone through the process of scrunching up into a ball, soaking thoroughly so it melted together into merely a lump of fibres, then caking dry for many minutes under the sun. And even if we manage to succeed in un-lumping that thing, as you call it, although I'm quite sure there's no such word, the ink might have washed away or melted into the pulp of paper. But anyway, enough of this depressing talk ... we have no other choice."

Fluendel stood up again and helped Anne up.

"Can I ask you a question, since there is plenty of time before we decide what we can do next?" he asked. They had started walking again without knowing which direction they were going.

"That's a question, yes," said Anne, stepping over a half-rotten log.

"What do you think this flower is? I've never seen it before," he said, holding up the flower he had studied so intently before.

"It's a shriveled-up daisy," Anne pointed out.

"Oh. I thought it was a new species." Fluendel looked shriveled himself. "Can I ask another question?"

"That *is* another question, yes," Anne replied, stomping through a pile of dead leaves and finding they were quite wet.

"Why is the ring such an important thing – I mean, who made the law that anyone who had the ring would be Queen in the first place? I wouldn't think a ... a plain diamond ring would prompt anyone to make such a rule whatsoever."

"The ring has a diamond in it, a real one, though rather tiny, and priceless –"

"It's a *plain* diamond ring, after all? What –"

"Okay, listen, I'll tell you," she said hurriedly, and continued, "I've read that there are three diamonds of ... of power, I've read –"

"You already *told* me that 'you've read' ..."

"Oh. Sorry. Yeah, okay. One diamond is, well, kind of white, like most diamonds, one diamond is green, and one diamond is red."

"Cool," said Fluendel. Anne looked at him. "I mean, fancy you had what you thought to be an emerald ring, and it turned out to be a diamond ring after all."

"Sure, it's cool," said Anne. "The ring itself is made of gold, and no one knows from where, but it is said that it was given by Firnale to Lilian, and from his grandson the tradition came out that the person who has the ring becomes Queen. Though it is a tiny diamond, its power is very great. I don't think I know specifically what power it has, though."

"Maybe the person who stole it wasn't aiming to be Queen, but simply wanted the diamond for herself? Since it's so priceless, I mean. You know, women want that stuff simply because it's beautiful and priceless." Fluendel received a haughty glance, showing that Anne had no mind for 'that stuff' as women had. "You're not a woman," he added, tactlessly, then added again, "but you will be."

"Wasn't it stolen before, then? It's surprising it wouldn't have been, after all, being so priceless and all that," said Fluendel, venturing to cover his earlier mistake.

"A wise duke attempted to steal it, once, but he failed."

"A wise duke? Why did he do that if he was so wise?"

"Because he wasn't wise. A witch cast a spell on him, and he became foolish and greedy, and now he lives in a hollow in a rocky mountain with some servants, counting his gold."

"Come to think of it, there was a greedy duke in the verse," said Fluendel, frowning and rubbing his chin.

They found that their direction had led them back to the lake.

"I remember something too," said Anne, looking at the waters. "Tepiraniel told me to find the ashes of water for they will show us the way to go, and I thought maybe they're here."

"Ashes of water!" said Fluendel. "How insane! The definition of ashes is 'the powdery residue left after the burning of a substance', and water can't burn – it puts out fire!"

"Yeah, that's what bugs me, but anyway there must be such a thing or else Tepiraniel would certainly have not mentioned it for me to find," said Anne, shrugging and sighing at the same time.

"But we have to find that to know the way."

"How very kind of her," Fluendel grumbled, "She might have just pointed out the direction instead."

"Anyway, do you have any ideas?" Anne said. "I have none."

"Same here ..." said Fluendel, "Um, maybe it's some special steam? You know, if water was not water, it would have burned, but since it's water, it can't help not being able to burn; it would boil."

"I think, if it was supposed to be a scientific term, there can't be any ashes of water, right?" Anne said, and Fluendel nodded. "So, in my opinion, I think the ashes of water may be totally metaphoric."

— CHAPTER NINE —

The Old Lady in the Thorn Bush

"Don't you think the ashes of water might be flowers?" said Anne by a sudden thought, looking up from examining a flower and giving it a sniff.

"Maybe," said Fluendel. "But what makes you think so?"

"You know, you can say that ashes are the result of great pain and difficulty, right? The seeds are produced and scattered by the wind, then it springs to life as a flower. It will wither away in an instant, but it gives many things before it does. Hope, beauty, happiness, and food for the butterflies and bees, which in turn provide us honey."

"A very good thought," said Fluendel. "*Much* better than my lame one."

Anne gave him a mock modest smile. Then her face froze.

"What?" demanded Fluendel hurriedly.

"I've just remembered a thing we have to do," said Anne in a hushed voice, indicating she was very excited. "We have to find a diamond. And Tepiraniel said I should put the diamond into this clam necklace –" (she yanked at the chain on her neck to show Fluendel) "– after I find it ... Can you make anything out of that?"

"Oh," said Fluendel, "Then it all fits! Now it's so very obvious."

Fluendel seemed to have deemed it as a premise that Anne was thinking along the same lines as him.

"What is?" asked Anne, hopefully.

"That the ashes of water must mean a diamond," said Fluendel.

"If it is so, so?"

"Then it is clear where it is," said Fluendel. "And we know where it is."

"No, I don't," said Anne. "Where is it?"

"Why, the duke must have the diamond since it's a diamond and he's greedy," said Fluendel. "And as for the duke, you said he lives in a crag in a mountain, and we know where all the mountains are ..." He saw the look on Anne's face and faltered. "Don't we?" he asked, then hastily changed it, "I do know where the mountains are, so no problem."

"I *know* where the mountains are," said Anne. "But then it doesn't make sense, does it? I mean, I thought we were supposed to find the ashes of water because we don't know where the duke is, because the ashes of water will show us the way, but if we are to find the ashes of water at the duke's place ..."

Fluendel seemed to have understood, since he too frowned.

"And then, come to think of it, I'm sure there was another task before finding the duke," said Anne thoughtfully. "And something about sulking witches, I think."

"'Find the diamond from the witches' nook, go to the mountains, find the greedy duke' ..." Fluendel seemed crestfallen as he saw that he had confused the idea within himself. "Oh. We're supposed to find the diamond in the witches' nook, and *then* go to the mountains to find the duke." He noticed Anne looking at him with surprise and realized why. "Did I just remember the verse?"

"I do think the ashes of water may be a diamond. I'm just saying it doesn't seem to be with the duke," Anne said, beaming and clapping Fluendel on the back. "Good thing you remembered."

"What's the talk about sulking witches?"

"Ugh, I thought, like, people sulk in corners, right?" mumbled Anne, scratching her head. "Well, I thought maybe witches need a corner to sulk in ..."

"I was thinking the witches' nook sounds creepy," stated Fluendel.

Just then, something on Anne's back shimmered. Seeing Fluendel's gaze transfixed on her back, Anne peered over her shoulders too and saw Belmer's golden wings, slightly fluttering.

"According to your theory then, it's back because I need it?" said Anne, and Fluendel nodded. "Seems very logical except for the fact that it appeared when I was poking the fire."

"Well," said Fluendel, "well, maybe I needed to see it so that I can tell you that theory."

"Anyway, that means we have to go somewhere. But only one of us can fly ..."

Choosing that timing, a single, pure white feather floated down.

"Oh!" said Anne, her eyes shining. "If this is the place Tulp once lived, that means there's also ..."

Suddenly, a shadow swooped past them, and a second later a bat-like creature with huge, feathered wings and long, eagle-like legs fluttered down and landed on Fluendel's head. Its chest was puffed out, looking like a robin redbreast, and it was making gurgling and cooing sounds while shuffling about, trying to find grip on Fluendel's head.

"Tha-that's a windlet!" breathed Fluendel, finishing Anne's sentence for her. He winced as the windlet began scrabbling at his hair, and he gently held out his arm. "Woah, easy!"

The windlet got the message and hopped down, landing on his arm and curling its strong, long legs around it.

There was another shadow, then another windlet landed on Anne's head, and Anne whimpered before holding out her arm, just as Fluendel had done. The windlet ignored the arm and settled down comfortably on Anne's head, like a seriously overlarge hen. That moment, there sounded many gurgling sounds somewhere above. As Anne carefully looked up, she could see high above about a dozen windlets, flying together like a flock birds do when the season changes.

"I guess these two flew down to help?" said Anne, offering the windlet upon her head a daisy. "Do you know where the witches' nook is?" she asked it, trying to look up.

"I've read that they know who you most need and where you need to go," said Fluendel, but with a doubtful tone in his voice. "I guess they know we need help, at least."

As if to answer, the windlet suddenly jumped off his arm and fluttered around Fluendel, nearly whapping his head in the violent action, and then the windlet laced his long legs under his arms and wrapped them firmly around Fluendel's chest. The windlet began to flap. Anne's awestruck face began to form into a smile as Fluendel began to hover above ground. Fluendel looked rather queasy. He closed his eyes tight.

"Woaaaaaaaah –!"

Fluendel opened his eyes and saw that Anne's windlet had taken hold of her in the same way and was now flapping vigorously. He looked below him.

"We're were flying!" exclaimed Fluendel, rather unnecessarily pointing out the fact. He let out a whoop, and Anne wondered if he had never flown before. Then she remembered that she too had flown for the first time only the day before yesterday; that it was amazing for one to fly even once in their lives. Taking a lift from the windlets was different from riding her wings; it was rather joltier, and painful around the armpits, because of the windlet's strong grip. She felt a jolt in her stomach, a funny sensation that she was falling, then she was boosted up again as the windlet flapped its wings up and down and sometimes glided.

"It feels strange to have short hair," said Fluendel, peeking down and breathing when he saw they weren't very high up yet.

"You know, Fluendel?" said Anne, her face cracking into a grin. "I'm no professor, but I think that's a very unique statement for a person who's flying for the first time!"

The windlets flew across the lake and swooped towards the waterfall. Anne and Fluendel braced themselves for another drench, but when at last Fluendel opened his previously tightly closed eyes, he noticed that they were through to the other side, yet they weren't wet at all.

"What ... what just happened?" asked Fluendel with amazement.

"The water just kind of went around us, like there was an invisible air bubble around us," gasped Anne, closing her eyes now. She was terrified, and was clutching hard to her backpack, which she had taken off for her windlet to be comfortable in grabbing her. She was sometimes even afraid to play on the swings, if they went really high – not that she was afraid of heights, but she was afraid of extreme belly-flipping sensations. As the windlets flew higher, though, even Fluendel was clutching his face, since he was afraid of heights.

When they reached the first of the clouds, however, Fluendel shivered and Anne found it very hard to breathe, so the windlets swooped down. Anne couldn't help letting out a yelp as her belly seemed to flip all the way inside out. When at last they had the composure to look down, they saw that they had come to the mountains that Fluendel had earlier talked of.

"Eh?" said Anne. "Why're we here?"

"No idea," said Fluendel, scratching his head. "I guess we'll find out, though."

The windlets landed at the foot of a mountain, which was covered with a forest, and there they gently let go of Anne and Fluendel. The windlets led them to a thorn bush before flying away.

"GOOD BYE!!!" roared Anne after them and was happy to observe the windlets looking back at her a last time. The sun was setting.

"Why did they lead us to a thorn bush?" asked Fluendel to Anne, peering inside the bush as if something might be inside. Anne was still looking at the two white dots indicating the windlets that was getting tinier and tinier.

"AAARGH!" Fluendel yelled, springing back and knocking Anne over.

"What is – yikes," said Anne, noticing the head of a rather shabby-looking granny sticking out from the thorn bush for the first time. The granny hobbled out of the bush seconds later, leaning heavily on a gnarled walking stick. She was wearing what looked like a knitted jumper and blankets, though no one could be sure with the weather-worn black cloak she had wrapped over herself.

The granny gave Anne one glance, gave a slightly muffled cry, then charged straight up to Anne before smothering her with the blankets in a bear hug. Then Anne recognized her.

"Granny!" she exclaimed joyfully, hugging her back. "I missed you!" Then she pulled back with a frown. "But ... how come you're here?"

"This is actually my home," the granny said with a smile at the look of incredulity on Anne's face as she gestured towards the thorn bush she had emerged from. "The home I invite you over to at the castle is ... well, a temporary house to use while I stay there, since I'm your mother's, the Queen's, lady-in-waiting." Then she noticed Fluendel. "My, Fluendel, you're the same as always – no surprise!" she said, hugging him too.

Fluendel looked as equally bewildered as Anne.

"Um, Granny?" said Anne slowly. "You know him? Fluendel and I have met only two days ago, so I can't see how you can possibly ..."

"Of course," said the granny.

"But I don't ... I haven't ever seen you before," said Fluendel. "How do you know my name?"

"Of course, of course, no matter," said the granny rather sulkily, as if something Fluendel said offended her. He and Anne exchanged puzzled looks. "Now come in, then! I noticed the windlets, and you must have come here with a purpose!"

She began to usher them towards the thorn bush. Anne thought that she had never before appreciated how spiky a thorn bush looks. Fluendel glanced furtively at Anne, and she noticed his eyes looked kind of pleading. Though he didn't seem to notice what he was doing, he was taking up a sort of chant, under his breath.

"I won't go into that thorn bush, I won't go into that thorn bush ..."

Anne said nothing and let herself be led into the thorn bush along with Fluendel. Once inside, she was surprised at how snug it was, with several candles burning giving off a pleasant aroma.

"This house is nothing compared to the one I had before, as you might have noticed – oh wait, you won't remember the house, but make yourselves as comfortable as you can!" said the granny, bustling them into armchairs and rapidly making tea for them. "Now, where's the kettle ... ?"

Anne and Fluendel made themselves comfy in their armchairs and waited until the elderly granny finally finished making tea for them all and clanged the tea tray onto the low, wooden table, spilling half the contents of the cups in the process. She herself settled comfortably in an armchair and began sipping her tea. She made a choking noise seconds later and as Anne and Fluendel watched concernedly, the granny spat out the tea.

"Dear me," she said. "Excuses, my dears, I'm getting older and I forget that my tea is around ninety degrees Celsius. Now, by what reason did you come?"

"First, Granny, is she safe?" asked Anne anxiously.

Fluendel seemed to be wondering who Anne was talking about.

"Yes, she is safe," said the granny, as if she had perfectly understood. Fluendel shifted in his armchair and listened carefully. "Tertalin is surrounded by the Feirns, but she is safe for now."

"Tertalin is surrounded by the Feirns?" said Fluendel, while Anne sat still, surprised. "But yesterday we heard the Feirns heading to our castle of Admon Loriens!"

"Well, it seems they are strong enough to strike two places at once," said the granny grimly. "Anyway, the woman who has the queen's ring is among the Feirns, claiming that she is Queen ... but Tertalin's walls and defenses are strong, as you know. We'll prevail, I'm sure. The King hasn't returned after disappearing the same day as you and Grace, and the Feirns turned up secretively that night."

"Who is she?" asked Anne. "Who is the woman?"

"No one knows, dear, who she is, or what her bond is with the Feirns," said the granny. "I'm not surprised the Feirns would use any reason, or no reason at all, to overcome Tertalin and bring down its strong fortresses. I'm merely surprised that the Feirns have returned, and, though I hope not, with growing force. A messenger was sent to them by the Queen, but even he didn't see her face, because it was hidden under a veil."

"It was Dad who stole the ring from Mum," said Anne. "He was planning to exchange it for the lamp of Tieral – with the woman you speak of, I believe."

The granny looked like she wanted to ask how Anne had got to know all this, but she did not question her.

"Your mother the Queen is much more worried about the whereabouts of the King, and about you and Grace, than about herself," she said, reaching for her cup. "Today is already the seventh of December. Are you aware that you have been away for six days now?"

"Yes," said Anne. "I've been counting."

"But then," said the granny, getting up to light some more candles, "where may Grace be? She isn't with you, I see. Maybe she got lost? Stranded? Wandered off alone?"

"No ... Not this time," said Anne, smirking as she remembered the time when the three, Granny, Anne, and Grace had secretly slipped into a market. Grace had gotten lost on her own, and Granny and Anne had found her standing by the lost and found stall looking rather forlorn.

Granny sat down again, and Anne began to tell the story of all the things she had been through, starting from the morning that everything started, from the time the King had slammed open the door when they were eating cereal to when she and Fluendel had ridden the windlets to here.

The granny nodded after Anne had finished the story.

"You need me to un-lump your piece of paper, I see," she said quietly.

Anne wondered how this granny could possibly un-lump their paper, but she stayed silent.

"I'm a witch, you see," said the elderly woman.

Fluendel was stunned, but Anne was more, since she was close with her.

"How come you never told me?" she exclaimed. "You certainly

didn't show that you're one."

"I can't pretend I did things to be proud of with my magic," the granny replied. "Can I see your lump?"

Anne got out the lump of paper from her pocket. The granny took it, then she pressed it against the table as if she were spreading dough. When she lifted her hands off, there lay a straight sheet of paper, with all the writing in place.

"That is *really* cool," said Anne, her eyes full of admiration. "Thank you!"

She reached for the sheet of paper.

"Look, you were right, this is the next verse, 'Find the diamond from the witches' nook, go to the mountains, find the greedy duke' ..."

Anne looked up at the granny, an idea clearly dawning in her mind.

"Granny – sorry – you said you were a witch. Maybe, if you know, you could tell us ..."

"Go to the west, and slightly to the north," said the witch. "Of course, it's silly of me to caution you about this, but it'd be better not to meet them, if that can be done. Don't mention me, if you can't help bumping into them."

"Were you ... in bad terms with them?" Fluendel asked carefully. "Are they evil?"

"Yes, yes," said the witch, "though not all witches are evil, like people would like to imagine, always brewing up trouble in their cauldrons they are constantly mixing and cackling on top of broomsticks – I wonder, who got that idea? People are very imaginative, you know."

"Do you happen to be one of the old people?" said Fluendel. Anne thought that was rather obvious, seeing she called the granny as 'Granny'.

"Yes, that's true," said the granny, looking rather impressed.

"Sorry, but what do you mean by old people?" asked Anne, since it didn't seem Fluendel had spoken of the old woman's personal age. "Do you ... do you mean something like before Lilian's people?"

"Yes," said the granny, looking impressed again. "Well, as I was saying, there were three witches who were called the Witches of the Nook. Now there are only two. I refused to work with them any longer."

It was a few seconds before the meaning of this statement sank in. Then there was an uproar between the two of them, Anne and Fluendel.

"You can't be!" they both cried out, jumping to their feet.

The witch smiled kindly, as if appreciating the surprise that they were showing. Then she observed the two for a moment.

"Maybe I should tell you more about them," she said at last. "The remaining two witches of the nook are my sisters."

Again, Anne and Fluendel were much surprised, but they tried to suppress the reaction.

"I was the youngest of them," she continued. "We were inseparable. But I haven't met them for over a decade now. We chose separate ways of life, you see."

She stood up abruptly to take away the tray and clean the cups Anne glanced at Fluendel, then followed Granny to the sink.

"Granny, thank you for everything," said Anne, standing next to Granny and drying what she washed. "But now, I think we should go on our journey."

"Now?" asked Granny, drying her hands on a towel, at first surprised, then anxious. "It is already quite dark! Why don't you sleep in for the night and start off tomorrow morning? It's a long journey from here to the witches' nook."

"Oh, Granny," said Anne, "I have to meet Tepiraniel in four days' time, and I don't think I can be there on time unless we go now – especially if the witches' nook is so far away."

"I see," said Granny somewhat sadly. They joined Fluendel again, who had stood up.

"Well, then, take care, will you?" said Granny to them both. "Come anytime you like, and I'll be here to welcome you. This thorn bush will never raise its thorns to hurt you, my dears."

She ushered them out of the thorn bush. Once outside, Anne was surprised for a moment at how dark her surroundings were, for she had unconsciously imagined the bright orange sky would still be there.

"Come here, both of you," said the old woman suddenly, and she pulled them close in a warm hug. Then she noticed Belmer's wings were glimmering on Anne's back, and that Fluendel had nothing.

"Oh, right," said the witch. "You'll need some perfume," she declared to Fluendel before disappearing into the thorn bush.

Fluendel stared after her. He turned to Anne.

"Do I smell bad?" he asked.

"I don't know," said Anne mischievously, but seeing Fluendel's serious expression, she actually sniffed at him, then declared he smelt rather good.

The witch returned with a perfume bottle. The perfume bottle was shaped like a teardrop, and it had clear liquid inside.

"There's only half of it," she wheezed, shaking the bottle so it frothed, "but it'll serve you well enough, I think. You don't have to return it."

Fluendel eyed the frothing liquid which Granny had shoved into his hands.

"You can wait till the frothing stops," said the witch hastily. "Now, you'd better be on your way then, for the journey is a long one. Goodbye!"

"Wait," called Fluendel before the witch could disappear into the bush again. "Excuse me, but what am I supposed to do with this?"

"Oh, yes," she said, turning around. "You just have to spray it on yourself. Like perfume, just as I said. It might be more effective if you spray it where you can breathe it in."

Fluendel meekly sprayed on the perfume. When he first began to float, he jumped up in surprise, which put him up in the air much more effectively. Fluendel looked rather horrified, then peered at the liquid in his hand, which was frothing again.

"You're flying!" said Anne, watching with an amused expression as Fluendel hovered above ground.

"I know," said Fluendel, "but how do I come back down again?"

He gestured frantically for help as he began to rise higher, and Anne quickly reached out to grab his ankle.

"Anne seems to know how to fly," said the witch, gesturing to Anne's back where Belmer's wings were fluttering. "Mind you, as a personal advice, I think this perfume method is more or less like controlling a horse, but the ride may be quite different ..."

She disappeared totally.

Anne flew up and caught hold of Fluendel's arm.

"So, you have any tips?" asked Fluendel, wobbling a little. "You do know how to fly."

"Well, Tepiraniel told me to think moving my wings are like moving my arm or something. But you might as well listen to what Granny said, because I've never flown with perfume."

"Right," said Fluendel, taking a deep breath, and Anne let go of his arm.

He was still wobbling, but Anne was surprised how well he was doing on his first try.

"Right, now where's west?" he asked shakily.

Anne got out her container of water and floated the model of a water petal upon it.

"This way," she said, pointing a little more to the left than the way the windlets had returned back to their home. She took the lead, and Fluendel followed her a little reluctantly, taking care not to look down.

"So strange ..." Anne heard Fluendel mutter. Thinking about it, she did agree, though she didn't voice her thoughts. It was strange to see him floating around with nothing visible holding him up.

– CHAPTER TEN –

The Witches' Nook

"I think this is it," said Anne at last. She and Fluendel had been flying non-stop from the thorn bush to all the way here. The sky was getting lighter now, but the wispy grey clouds that covered the sky kept the atmosphere equally gloomy.

"What is it like to fly like that?" asked Anne quite eagerly, after observing Fluendel for a while.

"I feel suspended," said Fluendel languidly. "I really am, I suppose, so there's no surprise there. I suppose this was exciting for the first hour, but as I am afraid of heights, this isn't exactly my idea of fun."

They began to descend now, rather slowly, because Anne insisted that they must be careful and make sure no one sees them. Fluendel wondered if it would be any use to descend slowly when they were already a few hundred meters above the ground and were obvious figures of people amidst the greyish white sky. If anyone was about, they'd be giving the person a chance to take a good, long look as they descended at a snail's pace. If this was supposed to be a joke in Anne's opinion, a *very* funny joke it seemed to be when Fluendel felt like he was slowly melting away drop by drop all the while they descended at that snail's pace.

"Relax a bit," said Anne serenely, confirming his suspicion. "We're *almost* there."

They could see a dark forest underneath them, and they cautiously landed in a tree. Nothing responded except a couple of crows that happened to be dozing in that tree. Anne involuntarily winced as the crows let out ugly screeches.

"Such a pity that we have to come here for the ashes of water," said Fluendel, whispering without knowing he was. "I would have felt *very* grateful indeed to Tepiraniel if she had just kindly handed it to us." They slipped down the tree.

"I guess the witches are supposed to be there?" suggested Anne, pointing to clearing where there was a cluster of huge rocks jutting out like miniature mountains. There was no plant around the clearing except for a few withering yellow patches of grass.

"Gosh," said Fluendel suddenly. "I forgot about my horse ... it's the first time I forget about my horses in a century! I left it at the waterfall!"

"Don't worry, I'll give a good guess that your horse has enough brains to find his way back home," Anne assured him. "We didn't see him when we were flying on the windlets, right? There, then!"

Fluendel didn't look much reassured, however.

Anne walked around, skirting around the edge of the forest until she came to the part nearest to the rocks.

"Supposing that these rocks are the witches' den or something, are you planning to just barge in?" asked Fluendel worriedly.

"Yeah," said Anne, "but I'm not barging in, I'm creeping in."

She was about to dart forward when Fluendel pulled her back.

"Just a moment," he said. "Are you sure there's no ... no curses? You might be hurt beyond what I can heal."

"Uhuh," said Anne unconvincingly, "not sure. You can heal?"

"What's the plan?"

"We creep in and hide." Anne turned back to concentrate.

"The end?" Fluendel looked as if he thought Anne was ordaining too many risks. But if Anne was to go anyway, he thought it'd better be two than one, so they both darted forward to the rocks.

They hid, though they didn't know where they were supposed to hide, pressing themselves against a moderately small rock, similar in size to the one Fluendel had sat on back at Admon Loriens.

"I think there must be a code or the like ..."

Anne trailed her hand along the rock. She suddenly yelped, jumping back with a hiss of pain.

"What's the matter?" asked Fluendel, examining her hand as if there would be some horrible gash, puzzled, though relieved, when there were none of the sort.

"It burnt hot!" she exclaimed, looking at the rock accusingly. Fluendel began to touch the other places of the rock. When he came to the same spot Anne was burnt, he withdrew his hand quickly, for the rock felt as if hauled from a furnace.

When he looked around, Anne was fumbling about her hair. As he watched on curiously, she held out a hairpin triumphantly and touched it experimentally on the hot spot. Instantly, the hairpin melted away, but then in the place that it had evaporated, there came a key hole. Anne searched for another hairpin.

"How did you know this?" Fluendel asked Anne in amazement as she now inserted the hairpin to the keyhole.

"Of course, I didn't know – I just guessed," she replied, as the hole gave a satisfying click. "But these hairpins I've got are slightly ... hmm, magical, if you call it that way. Specially designed for uses in picking locks, bolts and doors. So, why not a rock?"

With that, she gave the rock a little push. Her fingers went right through the rock. She felt very fluttery, with one hand dipped into the rock as if the rock was a waterfall which she could pass through. Then she remembered that she was about to step into the witches' nook, not some fantastical fairyland. She looked around and saw Fluendel waiting for her to go, but waiting to offer to go first if she wanted him to. She crouched down and crawled into the rock.

For a moment, she felt suspended in between being here and being there, wondering if she could possibly think if she did not exist in a place. It also seemed she was inside the solid rock itself, for she was aware of seeing the colour grey, without any brightness or darkness. Then she passed through. Instantly, a slight breeze played with her hair, and she could feel movement again, breathing the clear and fresh air. The ground was uneven, with grass that was sometimes withered, like she was on a hill, and fir trees grew abundantly. It was as if she had been there before, but she couldn't quite place when she had been.

The time of day seemed to have changed. For all she knew, she thought could be in a totally different space with different times of day. She couldn't decide if it was supposed to be sunset or sunrise, though she could see a glimmer of the sun between the fir trees.

Just as she was reaching for her water petal compass, Fluendel joined her, looking at her and around without a word, looking disturbed. He dropped his eyes to look at the rock that he had come through with a slight frown. Anne looked down at the compass in her hand. She too frowned. The tip of the petal was wandering this way and that, not settling. Though she held it very still, it did not rest on a certain point but kept circling around. She sighed with a raised eyebrow and looked up to meet Fluendel's eye. He shrugged, as he was apt to do. He seemed still deep in thought.

"I never expected the witches' nook would be like this," said Anne quietly.

"So, do you know if it's sunset or sunrise?" he asked.

"No."

They stood for a moment, wondering, Anne fingering the compass. Then presently she put it back in her bag and began walking. Fluendel followed behind her.

"I suppose ... we'll get somewhere?" asked Anne, and Fluendel nodded. She found it rather unsettling that there was no specific direction; no north, no south, no east, and no west.

"Does that mean that there is no axle?" Anne wondered aloud.

"Pardon?"

Fluendel was looking at her, concernedly.

"Oh, I mean ... nothing," she said, a little flustered

Fluendel and Anne came to a castle at length. It could be seen from quite a distance away, and as soon as Anne caught sight of it and identified it as a castle, she broke into a run. Then she remembered Fluendel and slowed down again.

"You are aware," said Fluendel, "that the witches of the nook might be watching our every move from any of those windows in the castle, aren't you?"

"Right, yeah," said Anne. The castle seemed to be surrounded by a wall, and luckily, they didn't have to wander around, looking for the gate, because they were on the castle side where the gate was. They reached the iron gates that looked somewhat very solemn.

Anne bent down and peered into the lock very carefully. Then she reached for her hair again for the reinforcements of hairpins. She soon had the lock picked, and they opened the gates with a low creak.

Fluendel and Anne hurried to the wooden front doors beyond the gates. The doors had iron door knockers on both sides. The doors were huge. Anne traced her fingers over the smooth stone arch and gazed at the weathered, grey stones making up the castle.

"You don't suppose we should ... *knock*, do you?" she asked. Fluendel nodded uncertainly, so Anne brandished another hairpin and studied the door. It had six keyholes in total. Anne look up doubtfully at the topmost keyhole, some place up nearly three times her height.

"Um, boost me up, will you, if you can reach ..."

"Your wings have returned, you know," said Fluendel, gesturing to her back, and Anne was relieved to see he was right.

She flew up and picked open the lock, then the one below, another, another, another, and finally, the last lock was open. Anne and Fluendel positioned themselves and each pushed at a door but found that it would not open. All it would do was to budge slightly, opening a gap so small that Anne could barely fit her fist in between.

"It's barred," she commented. "I guess we do have to open this door, since it is so securely closed."

She rummaged her backpack while Fluendel looked on silently, wondering what she was searching for. Anne pulled out a curious-looking metal instrument that looked like a short baton. She clicked the instrument, as if clicking a pen, and instantly it expanded until it was long and thin. Its tip was now sharp and pointy. She inserted that instrument and struck at the bars experimentally. As barely no sound was made as she struck at it with the metal instrument, she seemed satisfied and turned to Fluendel.

"Wood," she said, beaming at him. She began to work on the bar, pushing the pointy end into the wooden bar about two millimeters and pushing it along.

"Um, exactly how many hours will this operation take?" asked Fluendel, waiting by her side, unable to do anything helpful but to watch.

"Oh, I don't know," said Anne cheerfully, finishing the first bar. "There are two bars, I think."

She finished the bars in the next twenty minutes, and Fluendel checked the sky hopefully, but to his confusion, the sun was still hidden, nowhere in sight, neither up nor down and neither sunset or sunrise.

"Come on," said Anne, nudging him and arousing him from his thoughts. He pushed on his door again, and this time the huge doors slowly opened. When the door had open enough for the two of them to slip in side by side, they went in and saw that they were looking out into a rectangular courtyard through some high, stone arches upon a low wall, making wide windows.

"So, there was a reason my wings had returned," said Anne in a hollow voice. She looked down at the instrument in her hands and shoved it back inside her bag. They followed the open corridor down the right side reaching an open doorway. Through the doorway was one wide stone staircase leading up and another leading down. There was another open doorway to the side, leading to a wide corridor. Moving forward, they could see gothic style arched windows on the right side of the corridor, and great arches carved into the stone wall on the left.

Opening a door at the end of the corridor, they stepped outside. They walked across the grass, passed through an archway, and entered inside through another door.

"What are we supposed to do now?" mumbled Anne, wandering about, though slightly less enthusiastically, because they were not here to explore but to get the ashes of water from the witches of the nook. Fluendel didn't answer, maybe because he guessed correctly that the question wasn't meant to attain any answers. They came past another open door. Anne poked her head in.

"Fluendel," she breathed with awe. "I think this is a library."

Fluendel and Anne stepped into the room, both beaming at the many books. The room was fairly big. There were rows and rows of tall bookshelves in the middle, desks around the shelves, and desks by the windows on the sides. On each of the desks, there was a lamp, and open lanterns with burning candles inside hung from nails jutting out from the walls between the windows.

Anne walked about between the tall bookshelves, admiring how they all looked so old and dusty. On some of the bookshelves, ladders were propped up against them. As she moved around, she saw about a dozen books stacked upon one of the desks. She selected a thick, dusty book from the stack and opened it curiously. A parchment that had been folded into a little square slid out from it, onto the floor. Anne laid the book down onto the desk and stooped down to pick the folded parchment. When she had unfolded it, she could see elegant handwriting in ink written on the parchment in the form of a letter. Just at that moment, Fluendel passed Anne's row holding a dusty looking book which he was unconsciously rubbing clean.

"What's that?" he asked, noticing the paper in her hand that she was peering at.

"Looks like you've got one too, whatever it is," said Anne, pointing at a folded parchment peeping out of Fluendel's book.

Fluendel unfolded the parchment and peered down, and Anne resumed examining hers. It seemed to be some kind of language she didn't know. She looked around at Fluendel. As his eyes swept past the writing, his frown deepened, as if he understood what it meant.

"It's in a different language, isn't it?" asked Anne, as Fluendel started folding his parchment crudely and stuffing it into the book once more.

"Yes, indeed," said someone right beside them, in a croaky voice and a unique accent. Anne and Fluendel swiveled around and jumped because the person who had spoken was literally right beside them. She was an elderly person, quite tall and thin, with protruding eyes, and looked very capable of looking strictly stern. She was wearing a heart-warming smile at the present, however. She was wearing dark purple robes, and a matching hat. Seeing the parchment in Anne's hand, her smile faded a little.

"Oh, never mind that parchment, *dearie* me, we forgot to remove that ... *we forgot to remove that?!*" she exclaimed in disbelief. The lady frowned. "I thought I told you to remove it all months ago, but no matter."

Anne and Fluendel exchanged a glance, not understanding who she was talking to.

"We must introduce ourselves, mustn't we? I am Amirster, and she's ... she's ..." Amirster looked around and saw that 'she' wasn't there. "*Lutwin!*" she called. "She's Lutwin," she said, returning to Anne and Fluendel.

"You're not evil?" said Fluendel, then he got jabbed by Anne.

"I'm here!" cried a woman, appearing to have materialized out of nowhere, this time in dark green robes and a matching hat. She seemed to be almost exactly like Amirster, except for her voice, which had a different sort of accent. "Oh, hello, kiddos, I am Lutwin."

She did a slow, graceful bow. Then she noticed the parchment crammed into the book and sniffed with contempt. "Never mind that, kids, we'll have that burnt." She gave two snaps of her finger, and the parchments burst into flames, burning away into a pile of ashes without harming the book it was upon.

"You have come to get the ashes of water, I presume?" said Amirster. Anne and Fluendel looked at each other.

"By which reason?" asked Lutwin. "Surely, not greed ..."

"I have a quest to complete," said Anne. "And –"

Fluendel nudged her.

"Ah," said Lutwin. "Of course. You don't trust us, do you?"

She began to lead them out of the library, talking while walking.

"We, witches of the nook, were planning on something great, something very great. There were prophecies made about three children. We sought to kidnap these three children, in order to disturb the prophecy. Now, in here." She opened a door and waited for them to pass in. In the rather bare room hung three paintings.

"The first child was Gaudiel," Lutwin said, indicating to one of the paintings, where a blonde-haired girl was walking in a forest alone, her back towards them. Fluendel stiffened and grew pale, but stayed silent. "I was the one to kidnap her. She showed me that not all people are bad – that I shouldn't loath every race beside my own. Gaudiel forgave me, but she had to leave for the north-east."

"The second child was called Noctren," said Amirster, and Anne and Fluendel looked at a painting where a girl with dark-brown hair sat hugging herself in a dark corner, her hair hiding her face from view. "She was a sweet child, but she was so lonely, and there was a bitterness in her heart. She thought that she was loved by no one, so naturally it was easy to become friends with her. But she realized what my purpose had been. I felt so wretched when she left."

"This is the third child," said Lutwin, and they looked at the third painting, where another girl, with ash-brown hair and hazel eyes, was grinning at them cheekily. There was a shocked silence. Then Fluendel examined Anne, then looked back at the painting.

"It can't be," Fluendel said, "but is that Anne?"

"Yes, she's called Anne," said Lutwin, surprised. "Do you know her?"

"Why, she's right here," said Anne, looking at the painting of her younger self. The painting did look very similar to her. "I'm Anne."

"Good gracious," said Amirster, looking at Anne, her hair, and her eyes. "You *are* Anne!"

"I wasn't kidnapped," said Anne bluntly. "At least, I don't remember being kidnapped – but ... did Granny ... was it Granny, then?!"

"Oh," said Lutwin. "You call her Granny? Her name is actually Meilore."

"You kidnapped Gaudiel, and you kidnapped Noctren," said Anne, turning to each Lutwin and Amirster. "*She* kidnapped *me*?"

"Well, she did," said Amirster, carefully, "but she returned you to your family."

Anne didn't know whether to feel angry or hurt, or glad that though Meilore had kidnapped her, she returned her to her family out of her own will, unlike Amirster and Lutwin. She assumed a look of confusion.

"You were very young, so naturally you wouldn't remember very clearly," said Lutwin, placing a hand on her shoulder. "And Meilore has been your mother's lady-in-waiting ever since, caring for you, so you might have thought what you remember of being kidnapped as a picnic with her."

"So, do you perhaps trust us now?" said Amirster. "Even if you don't, I don't blame you, and it is a very good thing to stay on your guard against unfamiliar objects, but I trust you."

"And I," said Lutwin, plunging her hand into the folds of her robes. She brought out a small black box that looked rather like the ring box Queen Luna had.

"This is the ashes of water," said Amirster, opening the box and handing it to Anne. Inside was a golden ring, with a tiny, green jewel clasped amidst it.

"It looks exactly like the queen's ring, except that the jewel is green," Anne said, looking up from peering at the ring.

"The duke that I had cursed had tried to steal it once," said Lutwin. "About time, too, that the curse wore off, right?"

"You put a permanent one on him that time," said Amirster, her tongue tutting and suddenly looking very strict. "Not going to wear off, is it? Unless you're *dead*."

"Oh, yeah," said Lutwin, drumming her fingers on her chin with distraction. "What can I do about that?"

"No one comes here now, even to get the ashes of water, because they are so afraid," said Amirster, leaving Lutwin to pace around. Her strict look faded away. "I don't blame them."

"Aren't you lonely?" Anne asked. "Although, no doubt this is a great place to be."

"Lonely?" said Amirster. "Of course, we are! Especially now that Meilore has left us, that is. Poor Meilore; we have not met for so long. Tell me, how is she doing?"

"Oh, she misses you very much," said Anne. "I'll tell her sooner or later about our meeting, then she might come along or something. And I'd come too, with Fluendel and Grace, after this quest is over ... if you'll have us, of course."

"You will always be welcome here," said Amirster. "The doors are not barred against you."

"Thank you for helping us," said Fluendel. "We probably have to move on now, though, to finish the quest."

Lutwin stopped pacing around and came over to them.

"Right," said Anne. "I've promised Tepiraniel that I would meet her in three days from now and there's still a lot left to do."

"Then you must go quickly," said Lutwin, looking rather disappointed they couldn't stay longer.

Amirster and Lutwin went with them as far as the gate.

"A fine work you've done with these," commented Amirster, looking at the gate hanging ajar.

"Thank you," said Anne, looking very pleased.

Anne and Fluendel waved. They crawled back through the stone. The keyhole disappeared behind them.

"Are you alright?" Anne asked.

Fluendel hesitated, then looking at Anne, opened his mouth.

"Gaudiel is my sister," he said at last, "and like a bad brother, I had quite forgotten about her."

Anne put her hand on his shoulder.

"Hey," she said, "I'm sorry I didn't realize. She ... she looks a lot like you, and I'm guessing the empty seat next to you was hers."

Fluendel nodded.

"I know what I'll do," said Anne, suddenly fierce. "After this quest is done and over, I'm heading north-east. You can come or not, whatever, okay?"

"You don't have to go through such trouble," said Fluendel bitterly. "It seems to me that she chose to go there, and not to return." He sighed, shaking himself up. "Now we go to the mountains, right?"

"Yup," said Anne. "To the greedy duke."

Fluendel wearily got out the perfume. Anne looked down at the diamond she was clutching in her palm. She opened the clam shell necklace and put the ashes of water inside.

— CHAPTER ELEVEN —

The Greedy Duke

Anne fingered her clam necklace which now held the ashes of water as she flew in the damp, cold mist next to Fluendel. As they flew on, occasionally checking the water petal compass, Fluendel dozed off from time to time and Anne sometimes held on to his elbow to snatch some sleep. The air grew colder as the sun slipped away out of sight.

Night came and went. The air grew once more warm, dry and pleasant, and a little while later the first signs of dawn appeared in the clear sky.

"Oh, wow," yawned Anne, looking at the landscape as soon as Fluendel shook her gently awake. "Look, there's the mountain again! You think it's that one?"

"I don't know what I can think," said Fluendel. "Aren't you hungry, by the way?"

"I'm famished; it's been two days since something passed down our throats," said Anne. "And that's when I count the tea we had at Granny's, which wasn't really a proper meal."

The sun was beginning to spread its realm upon the land now.

"I wonder if, when we find the duke, he'll be courteous enough to give some ragged travelers food?" Anne stopped speaking to look at the many mountains that came in sight. She gave a glance at the thorn bush at the foot of the first mountain, where the kind granny lived.

"Has anyone been to the end of these mountains?" she asked. "Does it ever end?"

"As far as I know, it's mountains and mountains beyond mountains beyond mountains beyond mountains beyond mountains, but it still has an end."

Fluendel flew towards the warm rays of the sun.

"Wait, wasn't the ashes of water to show the way?" Anne said, fingering her clam necklace again. She opened it to look at the ring with the green jewel. "How's this supposed to tell us where?"

They were soon surrounded with mountains everywhere, like one can only see the blue sea if they are in the middle of an ocean, and now the sun had risen fully.

"I wonder how the duke gets his food and trades his goods if there are only mountains," said Anne.

"Can we ... can we rest for a minute?" Fluendel asked. He looked tired.

Anne pointed out a grassy patch on a mountain, and they landed there with stiff joints. Fluendel groaned and slumped to the ground, where he fell asleep straight away. Anne lay down too and looked around her again. It was fantastic and unbelievable that there was a place like this. Maybe this was how ants felt about a park full of pebbles. She enjoyed imagining what life would be like for an ant, because it was something she would never know. She too fell asleep without much trouble.

In her sleep, her dreams were at first calm and pleasant, but then it became confusing. She dreamt that it was morning, and that she and Fluendel had become sacks of potatoes which the greedy duke, who was depicted as a overlarge pig in rich robes, ordered to be boiled ... to serve them a meal. They were the guests being served the potatoes, but also, *they* were the potatoes. Anne wondered if all of it made sense, but of course it made sense, because it was a dream.

Anne woke up in a start and registered that it was dark. Then she registered that her feet were suspended above the ground, slightly dragging here and then. And she realized that she was being dragged along by two people on each side of her, with a sack on her head. She felt a jolt of fear, thinking perhaps her dream had come true, then mirth as well as relief bubbled inside her as she ascertained nothing about her felt particularly potato-ish at the present moment. The echoing of the footsteps made her wonder if she was in a tunnel. She tried to guess how many people there were by the footsteps and reckoned there were about four or five people besides herself.

"Fluendel?" she spoke, in an experimental, cautious voice. No reply came, so she decided not to call again.

"She's woken up," said a voice to her left, in an eager voice, to someone on her right.

"Have you woken up?" asked the person on her right to her.

"Yeah," said Anne, with her head still encased with a sack. Her voice seemed muffled even to her.

"If you wish, we can keep on carrying you, since you're not that heavy," said the voice to her left. The Left person seemed to be excited at all times, while the Right sounded gruff but not in an offhand manner, and somewhat outlandish. Anne stayed silent since she didn't know what to reply, and Left and Right just half-lifted, half-dragged her like before.

Eventually, she sensed that they had come to a different place, either outside, or otherwise in a well-lit room. Also, the echoes ceased, but now a regular 'ting!' and some mutterings came into her ears.

"You'd better kneel," whispered Left, and Anne knelt. The pressure on her sides ceased, and suddenly the sack on her head was whipped off. Anne looked around and saw Fluendel right next to her. He looked around too and saw her.

"Fluendel!" she mouthed with a grin.

Fluendel's hair was untidy as if rubbed a lot of time with a sack while sleeping, which was precisely what had really happened. The person Anne had named as 'Left' had a few freckles and orange hair. He looked not much older than herself. Right had retreated to the right-side wall. She saw that his stature suited his voice, with a kindly, ruddy face and stubby fingers. He wore a spotless, white apron and a cooking hat, and he hurried off, as if he had just remembered he had a menu to cook. She turned to look at the front. There upon a marble pedestal was a fat man in purple robes on a golden throne with precious gems embedded all around. He was kind of bald, and he seemed to have had a good-natured twinkle in his eyes, but it was totally concealed underneath a blankness, and above that, a twinkle of greed. His eyes were fixed in front of him where his hands were busily working, and a pile of golden coins occupied the space at his left-hand while stacks of the coins towered at his right. As Anne looked carefully, she saw that he reached out his left hand blindly to his left to grab a handful of gold coins, which he counted and stacked to his right.

"... Nine hundred and ninety-nine thousand, nine hundred and thirty-one plus seven, nine hundred and ninety-nine thousand, nine hundred and thirty-eight plus, ah, six, nine hundred and ninety-nine thousand, nine hundred and forty-four plus eleven, nine hundred and ..." He kept muttering numbers and adding them as he gave a glance at the coins in his left palm and estimated the exact number with outstanding skill.

Anne looked uncertain about what to do, then she cleared her throat. The duke looked for a moment disturbed, then he resumed his counting.

"Nine hundred and ninety-nine thousand, nine hundred and sixty-five...."

"Sixty-four, your honor, to your confusion," corrected a thin man sitting at the duke's feet since there was no space at the dukes right or the left.

Anne hadn't noticed him before, but this was not surprising; the man was half wrapped in the overflowing hem of the duke's purple robe, while his face and hands seemed to be painted purple. He was clutching a scroll so long that the top was lost somewhere beneath the robes of the duke while he unraveled more paper like a toilet roll when he needed more space. He busily scratched at it with a stubby pencil, and whenever that pencil broke, he threw it over his shoulder, snatching up another pencil from the ground before him. Anne guessed he was the scribe to the latest number of golden coins.

"Excuse me," she tried again, cautiously.

The duke looked up. He looked quite deranged, muttering under his breath the number he had stopped on.

"Nine hundred and ninety-nine thousand, nine hundred and eighty-two, no time, nine hundred and ninety-nine thousand, nine hundred and eighty-two plus eight," the duke said, grabbing another handful of gold coins and resuming his work. "Nine hundred and ninety-nine thousand, nine hundred and ninety plus ..."

Anne sighed, and Fluendel shrugged at her, and they decided kneeling was useless, so they began to rise.

The duke's goal must have been one million, because presently he stood up triumphantly, knocking the scribe off the pedestal and sending the pencils flying, and shouting, "One million! One million, that is! One million golden coins!" Then he noticed that Anne and Fluendel had gotten up.

"No need to stand up, you may as well kneel down again," said the duke hastily, "Certainly, if curtseying saves time, kneeling saves more. And time is money, so saving time is saving money. Now, one million golden coins!"

There was polite clapping from all of his attendants present. Anne peered at the enormous stacks of golden coins at the duke's right.

"That is ... one million coins?" she asked.

"One million *golden* coins, yes," said the duke, "Can't imagine how big that big number is, can you? Imagine then, drawing dots after dots in a notebook. To draw one million dots, it would take one hundred pages! Now you see, with one million *golden* coins, how enormous the value, how priceless it is! But I am making such a good bargain. For the last goblin-made sword, with the last dwarf-made axe available!"

"Goblins and dwarves?" blurted Anne. "I thought –"

"Well, it looks like you were mistaken, then, because here it is."

With a snap of the duke's fingers, an ancient looking sword and a rusty axe were brought in on cushions of red. They were laid on the pedestal.

"And, resuming my story, to that, a pink diamond the size of a basketball! A terrific bargain, that is ... well, no need to feel it's a pity giving away one million golden coins, because I've got much more ... and it's such a bargain – though I spent a month counting and recounting the amount to see if I hadn't mistakenly put in another golden coin, and time certainly is money.

"To speak of all my riches, it would take me more than a decade! Just look at all these goods, this marble pedestal with my engravings on it, my flowing purple robes, my thirty-kilogram crown over there, my golden coins, my golden trumpets, my silver platters and my expensive Dulhorte porcelain dishes! Oh, not to mention my hordes of diamonds and rubies – and did you ever see a yo-yo made entirely of ice? Well, I have fifty snowmen made of snow that never melts, even in summer! That is why the nickname is the snow of summer, I do guess. I have them displayed at the top of my mountain, *my* mountain! Well, truthfully to say, I had to put them up there, because one of the younger maids thought it was ice-cream and died upon tasting it. Serves her right, ha, *serves* her right – get it?! And, I am very sorry to say, I have just not managed to steal the queen's ring, though I would have liked to show it off.

The ashes of water ... It is so priceless, *so* priceless indeed, maybe the only thing I so crave but do not have, though I have attempted to steal it ..."

He looked at them as if he had just noticed them.

"My, my, that bow of yours is of fine value! I would bargain thirty-seven golden coins for that one. Fine quality, elf-made, and it looks like you are not a very ordinary elf to possess such a good bow ..." The duke eyed Fluendel somewhat suspiciously, while Fluendel suddenly felt for his back.

"You've taken my bow and arrows?" he asked menacingly, finding his back empty of equipment.

"Ah, the arrows could be three golden coins each too, the feathers shed by a speckled unicorn, the stem by an oak tree, while as the head is of iron refined twelve times. I've taken your swords too, also elf-made, and again, too fine for a normal elf," said the duke thoughtfully as if pondering a price suitable for it. "Anyway, you must be starving! Let the food be brought in!"

He gave another snap of his fingers. As the food did not come in instantly, he snapped his fingers once again.

"Food?"

Then Anne could hear a sound of boiling water and oil, as well as a knife cutting down on some thick meat, and some kind of door slamming shut after something had been pushed in. She could also hear a sound of liquid being poured out. Then suddenly, two trumpets sounded ("Ah, yes, those trumpets are made of solid gold, 24K!") and through the tunnel by the side, people who looked like chefs in their aprons and cooking hats came carrying first a long wooden table ("Made of one single tree, this is, a tree two thousand, five hundred and seventy years old – count the age rings in it!"), and then the food, in huge platters of silver and silver lids on top, which they majestically opened in due time. Huge amounts of steam rose the instant they opened the lids, and the delicious smell flooded the room. Smells of meat, of roast apples, of soup and garlic bread ... Anne couldn't help gulping, and her stomach sent her a growl. Then Anne identified Right from among the cooks. He was taking off his apron and hat, and he retreated to the right wall he had stood before he had hurried off.

As they sat wondering what to do since it didn't seem that such a greedy duke would give away anything for free, sure enough, the duke cleared his throat importantly and impatiently.

"Hem hem, now, I see you are totally famished, and your bellies are groaning for this plentiful food, roast beef, roast chicken, garlic bread, broccoli soup, and, I am very fond of spaghetti, as well as this elder flower drink! It is dreadfully tasty, you see, dreadfully, and I would give it to you if you tell me how this perfume works, and why you were sleeping on top of the entrance to my stores. Also, tell me how you knew the entrance to the stores. We'll see if you deserve some of my dessert, according to the satisfaction of your answers."

At yet another snap of his fingers, the perfume was brought, and the duke glared at Anne and Fluendel as if they were the ones preventing him from using it. Anne looked at Fluendel, and he just shrugged, so Anne got that as a sign to go on.

"Well," she said, trying to put on a gracious air in her voice, "surely you know how the perfume works?"

The duke's face swelled dangerously red for a moment, and

after the normal colour returned, he said tensely, "I don't know."

"You don't?" Anne pretended to be surprised. "Why, how do you keep yourself from smelling like you do? Oh, well, surely you don't know how to use perfume, I understand, since you don't smell very ... pleasant. Our palace is much better than this. Even our maids can tell at what times and how to use perfume ..."

"So, you mean," said the duke, with a strain in his voice, "that this perfume is a perfume?"

"I beg your pardon?"

As Anne put on her prissy princess attitude, beside her, Fluendel put on a face of disbelief at her before trying to play along with her. He fixed his face to look sympathetic towards the duke, as if he felt sorry the duke wasn't intelligent enough to use perfume.

"Of course!" barked the duke, flushed darkly in the face and looking very disappointed. "*Maid?*" he shouted, calling no maid particularly. A maid darted forward. "Have this perfume. Though it looks mystical and very elegant, it is of no use but as perfume."

Anne grinned at Fluendel before the duke turned back to Anne and Fluendel to hear the rest of the answers.

"We were sleeping at the entrance to your stores because we needed to see you for a bargain," said Anne, continuing to answer the questions.

"What bargain are you planning to make?" said the greedy duke, already leaning forward in eagerness.

"As for that, we will tell you later, but first, I will give you the answer to the third question. We know of all your secret passages, and since the passage to your stores is one of those secret passages, that is how we knew."

"How do you know all of the passages?" demanded the duke.

"Well, I don't have to tell you, do I? Be noble, and serve the food, will you?"

Fluendel couldn't believe how easily Anne was evading the point of the question. He didn't know what the bargain was. He could see the duke paling in front of them when Anne told him she knew all of his secret passages, but all Fluendel was concerned about was that now he was eating. If Anne knew what she was doing, Fluendel would follow her plan, and in the meantime his job would be to guess what exactly her plan was and stick to it as unsuspiciously as possible. He looked at Anne, but she wasn't giving him any hint. She was reaching for a slice of tomato to put it in between a small loaf of bread as well as a slice of cheese and some lettuce, and now she was munching away on her sandwich as she had no other care than to finish it. Then Fluendel caught the duke's eye, and Fluendel began to eat too.

"No dessert for you!" cried the duke, after he had eaten the main food. His dessert of a cup of ice-cream with a cherry on top was served to him. He looked very triumphant.

"No thank you, anyway," retorted Anne. "In our palace, we have three courses of dessert, and we have an appetizer before we start eating."

The duke nearly choked on his ice-cream, looking as if Anne had just punched him on the nose. He slumped down on his chair.

After the food was gone and the table had been carried out, the duke stood up and paced upon his marble pedestal. The scribe hurried forward holding a heavy roll of red carpet, and he unraveled it before the duke. The duke descended the pedestal at last with a majestic swirl of all his purple robes, walking towards Anne and Fluendel.

"Why is the scribe painted purple in the face?" asked Fluendel, seeing the scribe scratch his painted face carefully. A rash had broken out underneath the paint, and the scribe seemed very allergic to the paint. The duke glared up at Fluendel from down below with a disgusted expression clearly expressing, 'Insolent boy!'

"How, then, is he supposed to blend in with my splendid, purple attire?" he said, menacingly, stepping closer and closer to Fluendel until it could have appeared that the duke had been wiping his nose on Fluendel's chest. "He would totally ruin it with his ugly face!"

Then, noticing that he was a full head smaller than Fluendel without the height of the marble pedestal underneath him, he hurried back onto it with a humph and resumed sitting on his throne.

"Now, the bargain," he said, once again leaning greedily forwards. He drummed his fingers on the armrest, fixing his eyes on Anne with his jaw hanging slightly open. Fluendel heard Anne inhale as she forced herself into acting again.

"I have heard you want the ashes of water?" she said superiorly. She scrutinized the duke with folded arms, and the duke seemed to have felt danger to his authority, because he stood up to make himself higher.

"Yes, that is right," he said impatiently. "Is that what you are here to deal with?"

"No hurry," she remarked as the duke jumped up and down

on his pedestal. "Well, I have it here in this necklace." Anne unclasped her clam necklace held it up, letting it dangle from her hands. Fluendel frowned. Now, did she really know what she was doing? Then he caught the duke's eye again and hastily changed his expression into a blank one. But, why was Anne trying to bargain with the ashes of water? It was supposed to show the way!

"Anne!" he hissed through the corner of his mouth. "What are you doing? It's supposed to –"

"Snatch it from her!" the duke barked and Left and Right moved forward with expressions of severe reluctance.

"Stop!" said Anne, and Left and Right looked uncertain, stopping beside her. She looked at the duke in disgust. "You should know that your method is quite barbaric, and I deem you are a real fraud. I came to make a bargain, not to be robbed by force. But it won't work, you know."

"What do you mean?" demanded the duke. "And you two! Why aren't you obeying my orders?"

"Think about it," said Anne in an irritated tone. "I am a princess. And *you* are a duke. Then who has more authority?"

The duke purpled once more.

"But, as I told you, you won't be able to get the diamond against my will, so try if you must to take it by force."

She flung the necklace to the floor, and the duke stooped down and scrabbled after it. Then, holding the necklace in his hands and slightly panting, he sought to break the clam shell with the axe which was said to have been wrought by dwarves.

The duke cursed under his breath as he brought the axe upon the clam shell, but the clam shell didn't yield. He tried again and again, but those efforts were equally fruitless. Huffing, he finally turned to Anne.

"What is the deal?" he asked.

"Give us the snow of summer," said Anne. "And give us back our belongings."

The duke paused for a moment to register what she had said, and suddenly gave a harsh laugh. Anne faltered.

"*Give you the snow of summer?* No one can give you that! No one would *want* to, even if they could! You have to take it, you yourself. But I can show you the way. No one knows the way."

Then Fluendel understood the meaning of the poem and stopped trying to talk to Anne.

"As for the swords, I can give them back, but the bow and arrows have already been dealt with," said the duke with a malicious smile, "and the maid has just finished pouring the perfume into the gutter."

"What do you think will happen if that stuff goes down the gutter?" whispered Fluendel to Anne.

"Won't the ... stuff ... in the gutter go floating up into this cave?" suggested Anne. They grimaced at each other.

"But then," said Anne again, "it might be that the perfume only works on beings that have their own thoughts. Like you; you can move yourself forward by your will in the first place."

The swords were given back, and Anne was given back her precious backpack.

"I will show you the way, though I doubt you'll be able to make your way back. As for the diamond, give it to me now."

"I will give it to you as soon as we reach the place," said Anne firmly, "and now, lead us."

The duke snapped his fingers and Left and Right put on sacks on their heads again, and they spun them around a few times in order for Anne and Fluendel to lose sense of direction, but the duke spoiled it by making much noise in strutting off from his pedestal.

Once Anne and Fluendel had been taken out into the open, they were spun once more, and their sacks were removed. Anne could see why there was no need to cover their eyes. The mountains that surrounded them had no significance to her; she didn't know which direction led to where.

The duke was with them on their journey, for he wanted no risks, and to have the ashes of water in his hands as soon as possible. He was constantly eyeing Anne's necklace, or rubbing his hands together.

When the night came, the duke's men, including Left and Right, pitched three small tents. The duke ran about barking commands and getting in everyone's way. Then they ate dinner and retired into the tents; the duke in one, the men and Fluendel in the other, and Anne in the third.

Early next morning, they woke and had a light meal, then they continued on their journey. The bags that the duke's men bore was now visibly smaller, since everyone had lessened them the loads of two meals.

The sun moved higher up in the sky as they panted up some mountains. Abruptly, the duke stopped, and so did the men.

"We are very nearly *there*," said the duke, emphasizing the word 'there', "and the sacks are to be put on again."

Left and Right put the sacks on Anne and Fluendel's heads and spun them around wearily, for they were repeating the act they weren't enthusiastic to do too many times. Anne stumbled as they ascended a mountain again and slipped on the way down, but she did not get a single graze, thanks to Right, who held her elbow with a firm grip in his large, burly hands. Fluendel, it seemed, did not have such luck with Left, who was constantly yelping, "Sorry!" Fluendel muttered and groaned inaudibly, but still he mumbled that it was okay every time Left apologized.

When the sacks had been removed for good, Anne and Fluendel looked around them with surprise. They were in a beautiful garden, green and full in bloom – though the season was supposed to be winter, where everything appears to have fallen asleep.

"Now, I will have the diamond," said the duke, and Anne opened the clam shell in her necklace. She gave the ring with the green jewel stuck on it to the duke, who stuck up his nose with a gleeful smile and removed a ring from his index finger to make room for the ring he had just received.

— CHAPTER TWELVE —

The King of the East

As they wandered through the trees, suddenly Fluendel stopped.

"What's the matter?" asked Anne.

"I read about this place in a book! It's kind of what you humans call fairytales ..."

"You seem to know a lot about humans," commented Anne. "Elves have things like fairytales too, then?"

"Uh, yeah," said Fluendel. He seemed to be very much preoccupied, so Anne let him hurry on. "The problem is, I read about this fairytale, the one concerning this place, here there are messengers of the King of the East, and they are watching us this instance too, probably, because their purpose is to stop people from getting the snow of summer."

"Then you know about the snow of summer?" said Anne.

"The snow of summer stops death," said Fluendel. "For instance, you said your sister fell asleep by Epir's dust? She'll sleep on forever, then, and it would be the same as death. But the snow of summer can wake her."

"But the poem says we have to save a king," said Anne, then she bit her lip and was silent.

Fluendel looked concerned.

"I know what you're thinking," he said gently. "But that's what your task is, isn't it? And you're here for the task. If we get the snow, the king is certainly saved, and that woman has no right to claim your mother's throne."

"Yeah," said Anne, staring at the ground. "But what if he's already ... dead?" She took a deep breath. "It just seems that the woman knew something we didn't. She certainly knows the law of Tertalin that the person with the ring becomes Queen. She would also certainly know that the King has to die for her to claim the Queen's throne. But she is claiming to be Queen already."

"People say Adren died," said Fluendel simply, "but what's certain is that he became the next king."

"Right," said Anne, looking up with a weak smile.

"Wait a second," said Fluendel, frowning. "Aren't you the princess of Tertalin?"

"Yeah, I am."

"Tertalin is one of the Tenant Kingdoms, right?"

"Yeah. So?"

"Haven't you met with the King of the East, then, since you're the princess of Tertalin?" said Fluendel. "You must have, like, gone to pay respect or something."

"Nope," said Anne. "From a certain point of time, involvements between the Tenant Kingdoms and Finadel were cut off. No one went to pay respect or anything like that from that time on, and they were busy with their own businesses anyway."

"Unbelievable," commented Fluendel, shaking his head.

Anne could hear a stream trickling somewhere, but she couldn't see the stream, because of the many beautiful plants surrounding her. To their right was a red rose bush with a large, overhanging weeping willow. They passed through it, letting the leaves swing gently. On the left were presently two poplar trees, acting as columns to what seemed to be a maze cut out from the bushes. Then everywhere around, there were fir trees, with delicate flowers such as wax flowers, buttercups, cow parsley, wood anemone, and many other flowers whose names Anne didn't know.

"Look, there's Queen Anne's lace," said Fluendel, kneeling down and touching the flowers. "When did you become Queen?"

"Ha ha, very funny," said Anne, trying to sound sarcastic but actually grinning.

"Oh, gosh," said Fluendel, his expression turning into one of horror. "Anne, I'm so sorry, I didn't mean it that way ..."

"No, it's fine," said Anne, surprised. "I assure you I didn't take it that way, either."

Fluendel seemed at ease for the first time in a long time, picking his way carefully through the flowers. Anne nearly forgot it was winter, not spring or summer.

"Um, Fluendel?" asked Anne as they wandered around.

"Yeah?"

"It's winter," she said. "How are we supposed to find the snow of summer in winter?"

"I don't know," said Fluendel. "Frankly speaking, I don't think anyone has ever found the snow of summer after Lilian, and so no one knows how it looks like, or what it is."

"The duke has, though," said Anne. "We should have asked the duke to show it to us, then!"

"Well, actually, I don't think the duke has it."

"Do you mean he lied?"

"No," said Fluendel. "I mean, he said a young maid died on tasting it. One doesn't die on tasting it, I am sure of that. It is supposed to heal, to give life, not to take it away."

"Oh, so then he thought he had the snow of summer in his hands, but he was wrong?" said Anne with excitement.

And that was when they saw a glimmer in the air. It was only for a second that they could see a trail of gold dust, seeming to lead to the right.

"Hurray," said Anne. "I've got half a plan.

"What is it?" Fluendel asked. There was the golden glimmer again.

"First, the duke is foolish."

"I know he's foolish ..."

"Yeah, so he would have thought, 'Oh! There it is, the golden trail leading to the snow of summer!' " said Anne. "So, my idea is that we go simply the opposite direction!"

"Maybe," said Fluendel with a grin, shrugging his shoulders.

"But then, what are we to do?" said Anne, suddenly frowning. "You said there were the messengers guarding the snow of summer, didn't you?"

Fluendel shrugged again. "We'll just face that problem when it comes. We don't know anything about this place, or about the messengers, so there's nothing we can predict."

"Sure," Anne replied. The forgotten trickling sound seemed to grow louder as they wandered to their left, where all the various bushes and trees and other plants cleared out and was replaced by grass beneath, and huge but rather low beech trees.

They passed underneath the beech trees.

Just then, movement caught their eyes. They looked up. In an instant, they were surrounded by soldiers, all armed, but without any of them actually having weapons in their hands. There were about twelve of them. Everything about them seemed peaceable, except for the fact that they were soldiers.

One of them cleared his throat. He had greyish hair, brown eyes, and awkwardness that was clearly visible.

"Excuse ... me ..." he said, his hands neatly folded in front of him. He appeared to be searching for the right word. At last, he said, "Follow us."

Anne and Fluendel could not protest, and Anne didn't deem it right to attack such good-mannered soldiers who were behaving as courteously as captivators could possibly do.

As Anne and Fluendel moved along with the soldiers, who were keeping their circle around their captives, the beech trees ended and were replaced by a grassy hillside. They mounted a broad hill. When they reached the top, Anne and Fluendel could see that there was another hill. When they reached the other hill's top, they could see that at the bottom of the hill there was a vast ravine with rushing waters. On the other side of the ravine were great castle walls, beautiful gates and castles. Seeing Anne dropping her jaw, the grey-haired soldier seemed to smile.

"What you see are the castles of Finadel," he said.

"Finadel?!" exclaimed Anne. "We're going to Finadel?"

The soldier nodded, and Anne covered her mouth to do a silent cry of happiness.

Peering to the left of the ravine, Anne could see the peaks of the far-away mountains poking up from the horizon and the trees spread below them. When they reached their side of the ravine, the mustached soldier led the way down, and Anne and Fluendel followed, picking their way carefully, and they in turn were followed by the rest of the soldiers. Anne decided to name the grey-haired soldier 'the general', since the other eleven soldiers seemed to follow his lead. The swirling waters drowned out all the little sounds they were making.

The general looked at the strong currents and glanced at Anne. He seemed to make up his mind when he saw her. Then he looked at Fluendel, pondering.

"What's your name?" he asked.

"Fluendel," said Fluendel, fingering his hair again, as he had made a habit of.

"Can you manage?" asked the general, he too reaching for the back of his head. "Crossing the ravine?"

Fluendel stared at the general, his nervousness vanished by disbelief. "I'm an elf!" he protested feebly.

"So ...?"

"Of course, I can manage!"

The general looked relieved, and now he turned to Anne. "We will carry you, if you don't mind."

"I can manage too," said Anne, taking off her shoes. The general winced as Anne stood on the ground with her bare feet.

"It ... will be better if you do not get your clothes wet," he said.

"And the current looks a bit strong," added Fluendel, looking worriedly at her, as if thinking she was too little, and wasn't strong enough to cross.

"Oh," she said, cleaning her feet the best she could and putting her shoes back on, though she would've liked to prove she was strong because of the patronizing glance from Fluendel. She found herself wondering again about his real age. "Okay."

Once again, the general looked relieved, and he signaled to a soldier, who hurried forward. They grasped the other's right elbow with their left hand, and their left elbow with their right hand, placing a folded cloak on top to make a seat. Anne sat on the seat and put her arms around their necks, and the general and the soldier lifted her up. They all began to cross the ravine, the water coming up to the soldiers' waist. Anne obeyed the general and folded her legs, so that her shoes and trousers did not get wet.

Finally, they crossed the wide ravine, and Anne hopped down onto the bank. The soldiers and Fluendel were dripping wet, and Anne fidgeted her fingers, feeling sorry that she was dry.

The general led the way up, and Fluendel squeezed the water out of his clothes along the way. When they reached the gate leading inside the walls, Anne could see people, their clothes all clean and neat, walking about with their everyday routines, some with their bags, probably heading for the market, some little girls grouped around on the grass, linking the daisies they had picked. Anne saw that Finadel looked more like Admon Loriens than Tertalin or Quindeli. She observed a stone arch marking the start of villages, where there were rows of spacious houses and gardens in front of them, everything without fences. The paths leading to the houses were just simple, flat stones, like stepping stones in the grass. Peering far down a row, Anne saw through a line of sequoias a clearing with swings tied on to an ash tree.

The general headed straight towards the castle, some distance away. He sent a soldier to run ahead of them. Anne now began to worry. After all, she and Fluendel had been caught in the garden sort of place because they had been seeking to steal the snow of summer, which was surely the possession of the King of the East, the King of Finadel.

Anne enjoyed the peacefulness of her surroundings the best she could with the worries bugging her all along the way to the castle. Nothing was crowded or busy, while nothing was too spacious or empty, and everything felt so fresh, and no one seemed to be poor or in grief. Except from some people wondering at them then smiling when they met eye contact, everyone minded their own business. Some of the people who saw them seemed surprised, however.

The castle was upon a slight hill. Anne spotted a person with a newspaper covering his face and his hands grasped loosely upon the corners, napping in the sunlight. She couldn't help chuckling. They reached the doors of the castle, now. Guards were at the doors, and guards looked down from above upon the walls. The guards at the walls took one glance at the general, and they opened up the doors. As they passed through, a guard happened to meet Anne's eye and involuntarily gasped, at which his fellow guard nudged him, then saw what he was gasping about and froze too. Anne and Fluendel were led down some corridors and up a couple of steps into a hall, where most obviously Deilan, King of Finadel, had received the soldier's message and had hurried down with his guards. The King did a slight bow of greeting, and he mounted the seven steps to his throne. Studying the King, Anne saw that he looked to be around forty years old or perhaps even younger, but already he had white streaks in his hair. She wondered if Lilian would have looked like him. He surely looked like Tepiraniel, if that made sense, in a masculine way, like he was her brother. As Anne went through his details as she was brought forward, she was surprised at how similar he looked to herself. He had the same colour of hair, and the same colour of eyes. He also had the same skin tone. Anne almost laughed. Then the King saw her and stood up in surprise. When he did that, Anne really did grin.

"You look as if you could me my dad," she said, then she stopped herself with a finger on her lips, seeing how abrupt it would be. "Sorry," she said hastily, and she did a curtsy, which was somewhat hard doing without a dress. "Your Majesty the King, I am Princess Anne from Tertalin. It really is an honor for me to meet you."

Beside her, Fluendel gave a preoccupied bow. Anne glanced at Fluendel and saw that his expression was one of shock. He looked at Anne and looked back at the King. The King did a slight bow to them also. For a moment, there was a thick silence.

"Will you please follow me?" said King Deilan at last, standing up again. The guards that had accompanied him to his throne stayed at their posts, while the guards who had escorted Anne and Fluendel went to his side. Anne and Fluendel followed them through the door that led out of the hall, down a corridor and into a room.

The room they were led into had a cozy interior, armchairs with cushions positioned in a loose semicircle around a wooden table. There was a fireplace on one side, with a portrait above on the mantel in an antique golden picture frame, and a colourful rug lay in front of the fireplace. A servant came forward and started stoking the fire.

"I thought some privacy would be nice," said King Deilan. He gestured to Anne and Fluendel to take seats. They sat on the armchairs. The guards and servant quietly went out of the room.

"This meeting is quite unexpected," he said at last. "I should say there is something very troubling for a princess of Tertalin to have come all this way alone with Prince Fluendel of Admon Loriens, son of Beiron."

"You know me?" asked Fluendel.

"I know your father well," said the King, "and our fathers knew each other well also." He looked at Fluendel's hair and raised an eyebrow. "I should say you are very like your father." He now turned back to Anne. "I would be glad to help, anything within my hands."

Anne looked half doubtful and half hopeful.

"Actually, it's quite complicated ..." she said.

"I have time to spare."

Looking at King Deilan, Anne felt somewhat very reassured. She began to tell him all of what had happened to at last reach Finadel.

"If that woman wants to become Queen, then the present king must die, and I am afraid that my dad is close to dying right now," Anne finished in a hurry. She paused, hesitating, looking at the King. "I ... was *wondering* if ... if you could give us the snow of summer."

"Today is the eleventh of December, by the way," the King said. "But why were you so afraid to ask that one question?" He smiled.

Anne didn't know what she could say.

"Of course, I can give it to you," he said. "I myself have received it as a gift; as a gift to heal my people. What use would it be to me or to anyone if I kept it locked up forever?"

Anne and Fluendel exchanged both gleeful and relieved glances.

"Thank you!" said Anne to King Deilan.

"And also," added the King, "This may be a surprise, but ... but I think that you are my niece."

"Thank you for thinking so," Anne stammered, looking flustered.

"Then one thing makes sense, doesn't it?" said Fluendel. "You and your sister were able to untie the knot."

"But what makes you suggest?" asked Anne.

"It is a long story," said King Deilan. "Are you willing to listen?"

Anne looked hopefully at Fluendel. He smiled encouragingly.

"Yes," said Anne, eagerly.

The King nodded, as if bracing himself.

"Well, first of all, I must start when my younger sister was born," he said.

"My mother is your younger sister?" said Anne. "She can't be related to you ... She's from the Hortmon family!"

The King smiled kindly. His smile was so much like Luna that if Anne hadn't known better, she might have really thought she was his little sister.

"When the baby had been delivered by the royal midwife, I was told that she had died. My mother died a week later. A year after my mother's death, the royal midwife was caught in the act of kidnapping a newborn baby."

"Do you mean that she kidnapped the Queen's baby, telling her their baby had died?" said Anne, looking shocked and angry.

King Deilan nodded. Fluendel frowned.

"On investigating, it was known that the royal midwife had kidnapped newborn babies, using ... herbs to smuggle the baby quietly into her box of tools and ... herbs."

"She drugged newborn babies in order to smuggle them?" Fluendel said, scowling.

"Yes, and she sold them to families of couples who wanted children of their own," said King Deilan. "She said she had sold the princess to the Hortmon family. We searched for them, but they had moved away."

"But, say, even if the baby died, just like the midwife said," Anne said slowly, "there must have been a body to bury, right? Didn't anyone notice the absence of the body?"

"The midwife simply gave us the body of a different child who had died before," said King Deilan. "We named the baby we thought was our family Mona, and that's what we engraved on her headstone."

"Your sister's name is Luna now," said Anne. "But how did the royal midwife get her job, if she had been smuggling babies like that?"

"She was cunning," said King Deilan. "She kidnapped only a few. She was very skilled, you see, for no baby died in her hands.

When she delivered all the babies and kidnapped a few, there were still more babies delivered than in other midwifes' hands."

"What became of her?" Anne asked.

"My father was weighed down with grief and furious at the midwife, for he had lost both his queen and his daughter," said the King. "You would be familiar with cases when a king punishes the midwife if the baby or mother dies? My father, though in grief, refused to punish the midwife, for he thought she had done her best. But after he realized what she had done? Her punishment was terrible. She was locked up in the deepest dungeons, where sunlight cannot reach, with a mat of straw for her bed, all alone. A single month passed before she wasted away. Soldiers dug a pit in the forest and buried her quietly, so that no one else saw the body."

Anne shuddered. Fluendel patted her shoulder.

"Can I see your poem?" The King asked. Anne handed him the poem, and he read it thoughtfully for a while. Then he stood up. "If you will follow me, I will give you the snow of summer."

Anne, Fluendel, a maid, and a servant followed the King to a padlocked, wooden door. King Deilan slipped his hand into the pockets of his robe and brought out a small, golden key. He fitted the key in the golden padlock and opened the door. Inside wasn't much. There was a window with simple, white silk curtains on the far side of the small room, a painting of an apple hanging from the wall, and for furniture there was a lone, one-legged wooden table standing in the middle of the room. The servant walked forward and crouched on the floor by the apple painting. He started prying out floorboards. Anne and Fluendel peered over, and they saw that under the floorboards was a chest made of maple wood.

After the servant had lifted up the chest, King Deilan inserted the same key he had used on the door in the keyhole of the padlock. When he had opened the chest, Anne could see a glass panel resting inside it, cushioned upon velvet. The King lifted the glass panel up and held it out for Anne and Fluendel to see.

Between the two panels that were sealed together by silver, there was what seemed to be a six-petaled flower, but one of its petals was gone. The flower looked very delicate, as if one touch would melt it away. Each of its petals looked like Anne's brooch, and what Anne had thought to be a water petal. The colour of the flower was like clean snow, and it sparkled like a lake in the afternoon sun or dew hanging on a blade of grass.

The servant received the panel from the King and began peeling the silver off the edges with a wrench. When he had finished, King Deilan moved over to the table and lifted one glass panel. He carefully lifted up the flower and severed one petal off. The maid stepped forward with a small pocket of silk, and the King put the petal inside. He pulled up the drawstrings of the pocket and handed it to Anne.

"This is the snow of summer," he said.

"Thank you so much," said Anne, biting her lip.

"You told me you had to meet Tepiraniel in some cave today?" said Fluendel softly, nudging Anne. Anne nodded. She looked at King Deilan.

"Go on your way," said King Deilan, touching her cheek. "I

hope we meet someday – your mother, too."

"I'll follow you afterwards," said Fluendel. "Now fly ahead."

— CHAPTER THIRTEEN —

Epir's Promise

Anne flew hurriedly, all the way back to Quindeli, where she flew down into the underground cave through the opening. The sky was growing dark, now. Tulp and Grace were sleeping, the same as they had looked seven days ago. And there was Tepiraniel, waiting for her.

"Well done," she said, smiling. "Now, you have the snow of summer to save the King."

"My dad?" said Anne. "Is he hurt? Did the woman hurt him?"

"The woman did hurt him, and he is mortally wounded, but no fear," said Tepiraniel. "Can you hand me the snow of summer?"

Anne reached into her bag and gave her the pouch. Tepiraniel took it, then she waved one hand. Petals swirled, then cleared away, then Anne could see her dad, lying still on the floor. His state was so pitiful that Anne couldn't move. Tepiraniel slid out the snow of summer onto her palm. She turned to look at Anne, who was shivering and shaking with one hand covering her mouth.

"You are frightened that he might die," said Tepiraniel, reaching out a hand to stroke Anne's head. "You can trust me. However, this will be too much for you to watch. You will do well to turn around and close your eyes."

Anne did as she was told, though she still trembled. Though she listened for any sound that will hint what Tepiraniel was doing, she couldn't hear anything. Then through her eyelids, she felt a blinding flash of light. She quickly covered her eyes with her hands. Then she felt a gentle touch on her shoulder. She opened her eyes and turned around to look at Tepiraniel.

"Is it done now?" she breathed. "Is he healed?"

"It will take a long time," Tepiraniel told her. "It might take a day, or a whole year. But be assured."

When Anne hurried to kneel by the King's side, she was relieved to see that the bloody wound in his stomach had cleared away. His eyes were still closed, yet a shadow of a smile lingered on his face, and he looked as if he was inside a pleasant dream. Anne slowly got to her feet, then glanced at where Tulp and Grace were sleeping. She gulped and looked at Tepiraniel.

"Your father will be staying where I am staying until he is fit enough to live with you," said Tepiraniel.

"Thank you for healing him," she said. "But what is it that I have accomplished?"

"You have done well," said Tepiraniel.

"But not well enough isn't it?" said Anne, pacing around in her frustration. "What do I have to do? Dad is still in the process of healing, Mum is surrounded by the Feirns, and Grace and Tulp are asleep ... I feel so helpless and alone!"

Tepiraniel smiled, but Anne was unsure whether she liked to see Tepiraniel smile right now. Tepiraniel handed her a sheet of paper.

Anne took it and read what was written:

Princess and dragon will waken,

"They will?" said Anne. Tepiraniel nodded.

When to Epir is restored her power.
The red jewel taken, the fall of rust,
Noble Tertalin will not cower.

The curse lifted will be the end,
But a new evil is brewing.
Another I send, another quest,
Unsure but in final prevailing.

"So, I have to help restore to Epir her power for the Princess and Dragon to waken?" asked Anne, turning to Tepiraniel, who simply nodded again. "This poem is much shorter, but it's harder to understand ..."

"Princess and Dragon will waken when Epir is restored her power, and that is what you could do," said Tepiraniel, looking at the poem. "As for the jewel, I deem that you know what it is, and why it is connected with the fall of rust."

Anne nodded, gulping. "So ... how can I restore Epir's power back to her? Is it related to the red jewel?"

"The red jewel – that is her joy," Tepiraniel answered. "It was taken from her so long ago."

"How can I do this for her?" Anne asked. "I haven't even met her."

"You almost met her twice before."

"Did I?"

"The first time was when you were in this cave those days ago," Tepiraniel said. "In fact, Grace and Tulp are with her at this very moment."

"I hope she's taking good care of them, then."

"The second time was in the Garden of Pleasure, which was once the battlefield that Feridan fought his first battle against Lilian," said Tepiraniel. "She protects those grounds."

"Surely, there are enough guards!"

"You will understand that a person deprived of sleep will find nothing more pleasant than sleep."

"I think I understand what you mean," said Anne. "I have another question. Why wasn't I affected by Epir's dust?"

"Tell me, were you ever so affected by sleep?" said Tepiraniel, now smiling again. "That is also the reason why you are suitable for this mission."

Anne walked towards Grace and touched her cheek, then she also went to stroke Tulp's nose and bent to kiss it.

"You will find help in Admon Loriens," said Tepiraniel.

"Again," Anne said, grinning, finding her energy again, now that she had another task on her hands. "Well, I'll be glad to go there. Thank you Tepiraniel."

"Thank you too," said Tepiraniel, smiling back. She began to shimmer, and petals whirled around her from thin air. "Take care."

LOOK OUT FOR THE NEXT BOOK!